JESSIE'S HIGH COUNTRY HEART

A Dart River Novel (#2)

PATRICIA SNELLING

Published in New Zealand by Patricia Snelling, Inthelight Publishers.
Auckland
New Zealand
patricia.snelling.books@gmail.com
Website: patriciasnelling.com

A catalogue record for this book is available from the National Library of New Zealand. ISBN: 9780473483029

A big thank you to my launch team for offering your time and valued feedback. I want to thank Judith Little for her long-suffering, encouragement and editing support.

****

Harold Joyce Cover Art - Martin Joyce Graphic Design

****

Other Books by Author:
When Hope Went South (Dart River Novel 1#)
Missing On Kawau
Unshakable
Broken Web
Rescue Net

Disclaimer
The novel is written using British English with New Zealand colloquialisms or Kiwi slang

Chapter One

New Zealand 1978

It was six o'clock in the evening when Jessie Lee yawned and arched her spine, stretching out the stiffness in her low back muscles. It had been a long day. She'd been leaning over the surgery's treatment bench attending small animals from early in the morning. Lately, she'd started to weary of her role as a vet at the suburban veterinary clinic in the Waikato. She'd had enough of dealing with small pets, though she loved them.

An ache stirred within whenever she thought of her friend, Hope Rigby who had gone to live in the Southern Alps in the remote rural village of Glenorchy. Jessie thought of her old school friend often. Hope had not only fallen in love with her father's top ranch hand, but the North Island girl also had a love affair with the high country.

The pure mountain air and alpine lifestyle appealed to Jessie too. Especially when riding along Dart River on horseback. But she'd been too busy to get away for holidays in Glenorchy since Hope had married Cole Rigby, even though they'd both invited her to stay at their home on Hope's family ranch.

But now Jessie needed a break. Change was in the air—and a complete change, at that. It was time to take a well-earned holiday, and where could there be a better place but Hope's stamping ground in the far south. How she missed the horse rides with her friend along Dart River and picnics with her at Diamond Lake. But nothing had ever been the same since Hope married Cole and that was why Jessie had not been back to Glenorchy. She didn't want to encroach on the newlyweds' privacy.

But Hope had missed Jessie too and wrote her a letter to invite her to come and stay...

Dear Jessie

Mum and Dad have asked if you'd like to come and stay in their ranch house in two weeks as they are going to go on a bit of a road trip in their motor home. Cole and our ranch hand and I will be keeping the farm going. My folks don't like to leave the house empty so that would be great—you'll have it all to yourself. You won't be intruding, honestly. They'll be away for a month. Please think about it and let me know as soon as you can.

Looking forward to hearing from you

Love Hope

***

Jessie looked forward to seeing her young brother. Tom had decided not to go to university in Massey. Instead, he had stayed to partner up with his father on their sheep farm in Bethlehem. They'd stopped running cattle and had decided that sheep would be easier, but it was proving not so, especially with the recent drought. She'd worried about the strain her parents were under running the farm. Tom was pretty clued up, as he'd almost completed an agricultural degree by distance study while working with his father. Now Jessie didn't have to feel guilty about not returning home to help them out. Tom had also been riding her beloved horse, Rusty, as she'd been fretting about leaving the animal behind when she first left home to pursue her veterinary studies.

What kept calling her back to Glenorchy? It couldn't have been the rural life as she'd spent all her life on a farm. Was it just her friendship with her old school friend, Hope? She'd made plenty of friends in the Waikato—in fact, she hungered for relief from the hectic social life of the veterinary fraternity in the Waikato province.

***

Jessie's work day had ended. She left the locking up of the clinic after a long, hot day to the receptionist and wandered out to the backyard. She sat down on the bench under the cherry tree and looked at the view of Mount Pirongia which she had always enjoyed when she had first started working there. Last winter there had been snow on the mountain range but it was nothing compared to the Alps. Now the landscape had become too familiar and was no longer a novelty. They were mere hills compared to the spectacular Southern Alps in Glenorchy.

That was it! She realised the magnet which drew her to the high country, the ache on her heartstrings. That's why she wanted to resign from her job each day.

It was the mountains that called her. The feelings were strong. They evoked wistful memories of her climbing days as a college student. She'd spent many weekends driving to Tongariro National Park with her father and brother learning the art of mountaineering and continued the activity during her university years. Each time she went to stay at Dart River Ranch with Hope Rigby and her family, the call of the mountains stirred inside her again. The yearning returned.

Now she faced a dilemma—whether to accept the offer from the veterinary practice to come aboard as a business partner or leave the Waikato for the mountains. What will it be?

She prayed, *Please God, lead me, and guide me in this decision. Please give me the knowledge of your will for me, and the power to carry that out.*

Chapter Two

The small church in Glenorchy started to empty out. As Hope Rigby and her husband, Cole walked towards their old red Chevy pickup Max their local vet approached them.

'How's that young filly of Misty's I delivered? I see you've started showing her this season.'

'Hi, Max. Yeah, she's following in her mother's footsteps. So wonderful to ride and a great dressage horse.'

'Actually, I wanted to let the two of you know I'm retiring next month. My wife wants to do some touring with our new motorhome and I'm getting a bit worn-out. We don't get enough time off to spend with our grandchildren in Christchurch. I don't suppose you know of any young vets looking for work who might want to locate to this area? It's just that it's pretty hard to get anyone out here.'

Cole shot a glance at his wife. 'Hope has a vet friend who has been thinking about moving this way. We could find out for you.'

'What skills has he got? Is he a farm or a city vet?' Max leaned on the bonnet of the Chevy.

Hope looked sideways at Cole and cleared her throat.

'Ah, well actually my friend is a woman, a very capable vet. She grew up on a farm and has worked with large animals working alongside her father.'

Max set his jaw and looked back at Hope. He tightened his thick lips.

'Oh, I don't know about a woman—particularly since she hasn't handled large stock on her own before.'

Hope braced herself against the passenger door jutting her head forward. 'Jessie has plenty of experience. I used to spend holidays on her parents' farm. During the calving and lambing season, I watched while she assisted her father with some complicated births, some of which were twins.'

'Oh, that sounds promising,' said Max, jotting this down on his notebook.

Their local vet told her that she'd handled them expertly. She often shared her experiences with me.'

'Is that so? Well, if you and Cole can recommend her, she must be alright. Tell you what—you ask her to send her resume to me and I'll look at it and arrange an interview with her. How's that?' He pushed the notebook back into his jacket pocket.

Hope rushed towards him, appearing to want to throw her arms around him but pulled back and just shook his hand.

'Honestly, Max, you won't be disappointed. She's an amazing person and has plenty of experience handling horses too. I'll phone her tonight.'

***

Dear Hope

Please thank your folks for asking me to house sit. I've been able to take the leave owing to me and extended it to a month. I just can't wait to go riding with you along the Dart River and out to Diamond Lake.

Your phone call about your vet, Max Greaves retiring came at exactly the right time as my boss has been pressuring me into making a decision about becoming a partner in their practice.

I have my papers and resume ready to show Max. Now that I have been thinking about it and the possibility of becoming your local vet down there, I would be so disappointed if he chose not to offer me the position. So I hope you bolstered my image plenty.

Haha, just joking. I can't wait to get to Glenorchy. Thanks for offering to pick me up from the airport.

See you soon
Love Jessie

A week later, Jessie's boss, Peter Cranston approached her again.

'I'm sorry Jessie, but I can't wait for your decision any longer. The board wants to make a choice by the end of this month and we gave you the first option as we don't want to lose you.'

He spoke as though he had a plum in his mouth, giving him an ostentatious air, but he was a kind and humble man and Jessie had found him to be a great person to work with. He had mentored her ever since she had joined the practice and she knew he would be unhappy to see her resign.

'I'm taking the leave that's owing to me and return at the conclusion of the month with a decision. If I decide before then, I promise I'll phone you to let you know. I'm off to stay on a high country ranch in Glenorchy. My friend's parents have asked if I'd house sit for them.'

'Goodness, you do get around. I know you're young and free and have the whole world at your doorstep. I'll wait for your decision with bated breath.' He gave a half-laugh, but Jessie could see moisture in his eyes as if he knew she was going to fresh pastures.

***

Jessie's flight had been delayed, so Hope sat at a coffee kiosk sipping a second cup of espresso. At last, her friend veered around the corner of the aisle pushing a trolley loaded with an oversized suitcase.

'Jessie! I'm over here.' Hope waved at her again. 'Is that all your luggage? It's so great to see you.' They hugged. 'You're looking good. The car's parked outside in the drop-off zone.'

Jessie laughed as she approached the car, recalling when she had seen Hope's bright yellow car for the first time.

'Oh, you still have Sunflower.'

'Yep, and she's going like a bomb. The mechanic says she could keep going for my lifetime, but I'm not so sure about that.'

Hope couldn't stop talking the whole trip back to Glenorchy, but Jessie struggled to keep her eyes open after a hectic week at the short-staffed clinic. She opened her passenger window and took some deep breaths. She knew she'd have to stay awake to help keep Hope alert driving around the narrow bends on the country roads.

Jessie pulled a letter from her handbag. 'I forgot to tell you, I received this before I left. A letter from your vet, Max. He wants me to meet with him next week.'

***

After a two-hour drive, they arrived at the ranch. Jessie couldn't believe she had the whole house to herself. Hope's parents' knew her well, since the girls had been at school together in Bethlehem and they trusted her to take good care of their home. Hope and Cole lived in the farm cottage in the field over the fence—an old cottage they had both renovated with assistance from Joel, Hope's father.

Jessie was placing the last of her garments in the empty drawers when there was a knock at the door.

'Sorry, I know you need a bit of time to freshen up, but we're putting on the barbeque. Mum left us some lamb steaks to finish up if you'd like to pop over in an hour.' Hope handed her a small bunch of wildflowers.

'Sure, I'd love to. See you there at seven. I might just lie down until then.'

Hope wandered out the back door and Jessie popped the flowers into a vase then crashed onto her bed. She focused on her breathing, inhaling the stillness, apart from the odd lamb calling for its mother. She gained a sense of security from the farm sounds which triggered memories of growing up in the country.

Later that evening, after the barbeque and a stomach full of alcohol-free cider that Myra, Hope's mother had left for them,

Jessie had to excuse herself to retire early. The flight, the lively conversations on the way back from the airport and the heavy meal had made her eyelids heavy. Sleep took her by surprise.

She awakened the next morning to busy farm noises, but her sleep had been deep and uninterrupted. Casey, the border collie, rushed into the house to greet her when she opened the front door. Myra had left plenty of food in the pantry for her and although Hope and Cole had said she was welcome to eat with them anytime, it was her choice to remain independent.

Later that morning she accompanied Hope to the stables to check out her mare's filly, Marvella. She was born charcoal black, and during the last three years, her colour had turned grey, almost white, which Jessie knew was usual for the foals of grey mares. Marvella, a beautiful Arab had a soft nature like her mother. She hadn't seen her since she was a foal and the filly was still black then.

'She sure has grown—a real beauty like Misty,' said Jessie as she leaned over the stable door.

'You can ride Misty when we go along the Dart and I'll take Marvella. Misty knows the river bed really well but I'm still training this young filly. She baulks sometimes.'

'Sure, sounds good. I'll help you go and get them.'

'No need to—they're all bridled and waiting in the stables. Cole saddled them up for us. He has gone to help a local rancher present a stallion to one of his mares.'

The two friends trotted their horses along the side of the riverbank, now and then stopping to take in the awesome views of Mt Earnslaw and the wild birds. Overhead a large Kea flapped its wings displaying red, green and gold feathers.

This is what she'd looked forward to when she took her holidays at Dart River Ranch with Hope.

But her mind kept drifting. What if Max decided not to choose her to replace him? Jobs for vets in that district were scarce. Max had been the local vet for thirty years and they didn't welcome female ones. Jessie was in for much opposition but she was already prepared for that. It did not thwart her, at least not yet.

'Come on—let's go for a ride through that shallow part of the river. The horses love it.' Hope gently urged Marvella on. The horses frolicked in the water. For Jessie, it was like old times.

Cole was waiting at the gate when they arrived back at the ranch. He looked at his watch and stammered somewhat as he spoke. 'I was getting a bit worried, Hope. I thought you were only going for the morning. Leave the horses—I'll hose them down for you.'

The girls jumped off their backs and handed the reins to Cole.

'You're looking a bit peaky, love. Perhaps you need to have a lie down before dinner. I'm going to stoke up the barbeque later.'

'Don't worry so much, Cole. I'm fine, really I am.'

Jessie glanced at Hope and could see the pallor in her porcelain-like cheeks. Perhaps she is sickening for something, she thought.

As evening fell, and they had finished their meal, Hope wandered back to the ranch house with Jessie while Cole offered to stay at the cottage and clean up the mess from the barbeque.

'He's quite the gentleman, isn't he? A real catch—and you both still appear to enjoy married life. Come on in for a quick cuppa before you turn in if you like.'

'I'd rather have some of that Milo drink Mum has in her pantry. It's nice with hot milk.'

The girls sat at the dining table sipping their hot drinks that Jessie had prepared.

'To be honest, I've noticed you're looking a bit pale these days—not like the last time I was down here. You're not getting any headaches or post-concussion from your old head injury are you?' Jessie squinted her eyes, focusing on Hope's face.

'No—you mean my fall from Misty when I first came to live here. Heavens no, I'm completely over that. Look ... I wasn't going to say anything as it's a bit soon, but I'm going to have a baby, that's all.'

Jessie almost dropped her cup, spilling a little in her lap.

'Ow, clumsy me. Well, that is certainly a big surprise.'

'Wait on ... I'll get you a wet cloth. Did you burn yourself?'

'It's okay, just a few drips. How far are you?'

'Only a few months. I'm getting that horrible morning sickness.'

Hope handed Jessie a cloth. 'We weren't going to say anything until the first scan but that won't be until next month. The midwife is sure everything is tickety boo.'

'That's wonderful news, but you shouldn't have been trotting, when we were riding along the river.'

'The midwife says it shouldn't be a problem.'

'I think you should just walk Marvella next time, or better still, ride Misty. She's a bit quieter.'

'Yes, Mum,' she laughed.

Cole came to the ranch house and walked Hope back home to their cottage later that evening.

Jessie lay in bed that night thinking how times were changing and wondering what kind of adventures awaited her. She imagined herself as the local vet building up her business around the Rees and the Dart valleys. She remembered Cole had said he was going to get Max to assist with one of the mares about to foal. In spite of having a head full of all kinds of plans for her possible new career, she fell asleep.

***

Jessie had finished helping Hope feed the horses in the stables and hung around playing with some foals.

'I've really missed this, you've no idea. Especially the smell of the mountain air and the views from up there.' She pointed towards Paradise where they'd been riding early that morning. 'I can't believe I've been here a week already. Max is coming to see me this afternoon, by the way. I forgot to tell you he rang me last night.'

Jessie lifted the bag of horse feed pellets and placed them on the shelf before walking back to the house. 'I'd better go back inside and check that all my documents are in order.'

'That's okay. I'm dying to hear all about it. We'll be in the ranch house during your interview and you can take him out under the umbrella on that garden table if you like. We'll make some coffee inside and bring it out. Just so you don't feel vulnerable here alone with him.'

'Ah, thanks, I would really appreciate it.'

Chapter Three

The meeting with Max wasn't really a proper job interview. Jessie had guessed he'd already made up his mind on Cole and Joel's recommendations and she had excellent credentials. This woman was too good to pass by, even in Glenorchy.

Max handed Jessie back her document folder and stood up ready to leave.

'I don't suppose you could get back to me with an answer by the end of the month. It's just that the position I'm in is a bit awkward now that they are offering me a partnership in the business. I have to notify the Practice Manager in two weeks.'

'Look here, young lady. Do you think I'm going to let you escape? You've no idea how difficult it has been to get hold of a young vet with your experience and qualifications. We've been really scraping the bottom of the barrel.'

Jessie's heart pumped loudly against her eardrums. Was she hearing correctly? Her stomach churned with anticipation.

'Sorry, what did you say? I didn't quite grasp what you meant.' She tugged at the hair behind her right ear, a common habit when she was nervous.

'What I mean is—when can you start?'

Her mouth dropped wide open. The thick portfolio Max had handed back to her left her hand and dropped to the floor.

'Are you offering me the position, really?' Embarrassed, she rushed to the floor and scooped up the documents before Max bent to help her.

'I recognise a skilled professional when I see one. Sorry, but I have to confess I actually know one of those clinicians you work with who has recommended you. I do need to run this past the Board of Directors for the Veterinary Cooperative in Queenstown. They'll want to check your credentials, so I can let you know for sure by the end of the week.'

'Oh, so you have contacted my clinic already?'

'Don't worry, they guessed you were looking further afield or you wouldn't have been delaying and holding off from giving your boss an answer.'

The end of the week couldn't come quick enough for Jessie. She was restless each day and Hope did her best to keep her occupied.

Awakening one morning to a knock on her bedroom door, she stumbled to open it, half asleep. Hope stood there all smiles and rearing to go.

'If you're interested, I was hoping I could take you out to Diamond Lake on the horses later today,' Hope said. 'I've got some stuff to tell you that might put a smile on your face.'

Jessie was up but not quite awake. She stood at the door in her nightwear, scratching her head and yawning.

'Sounds interesting. What time do you plan to go?'

'Cole and Mack are having to shift some sheep to another paddock by horseback. I need to move some horses so you could help me do that if you like. I've packed a picnic lunch to take to the lake after that.'

'Mack ... isn't that Mack whom I met at your twenty-first? We had a few dances together. He kept asking when I was coming down to stay with you again. He was up north shearing the last few times I came here.'

'Yep, he had substantial sheep shearing contracts around the country and used to go away a lot. But he doesn't do that much shearing anymore, except the animals on his own farm.'

'His farm? Oh, that's right. Last time I spoke to him he was looking for land.'

'Well, he managed to buy a hundred acres, a small holding for around here and is trying to convert an old barn into a farmhouse on his own.'

Jessie's face turned pink. She pulled nervously at her fringe. 'That's a lot of work—good for him. I'll just jump into the shower and meet you at your place in half an hour.'

Jessie didn't mean to cut her friend off short but the conversation was beginning to make her feel uncomfortable for some reason.

She couldn't believe what she was seeing when they had arrived at Diamond Lake. Were her eyes deceiving her? On the other side of the lake was a scene she'd not witnessed for several years. The wild horses were back, at least the ones that were left behind.

'Look, they are the remains of the Kaimanawa herd that escaped from that rancher, aren't they?'

'Yeah, they are the ones Dad had to leave behind during the muster when I had my accident. That ex-army officer Captain Richardson trucked them down here when he tried to start a horse ranch. They're the horses that broke free when his ranch hands didn't shut the stock pen fast enough. They're the last of the herd unless there are some foals we don't know about.'

'I remember you wrote and told me that they're now preserved by the Protection of Feral Horses Bill. It's good to see them roaming about here.'

It was peaceful by the lake. Usually, there were tourists scattered around the shore, but this time the girls were the only ones apart from a family having a picnic on the other side.

'Wow, this reminds me of the times we had when I used to come down from university. We would lie on the grass and talk for hours. I've missed this so much. I love the view of Mount Alfred from here. Doesn't it look amazing?' Jessie took out her camera for a quick snapshot.

They sat on the ground finishing their sandwiches and cold drinks while the horses munched on the fresh grass while tethered to a log.

'I can't wait to get down here. I hope I can do this community justice though—I mean it might be difficult to follow in Max's footsteps after all these years,' said Jessie.

'Don't worry about that. You have to be your own person and you're going to bring unique skills and qualities to the role.'

'Yes, I know. It's just that I read somewhere that some of these rural close-knit communities in this part of the country often show prejudice against female vets.'

'Look, Jessie. My father and Cole are totally in support of a woman vet and will completely back you up. Please believe me. You will do just fine.'

'Thanks, Hope. Hey—you were going to tell me something, remember?' She sat back on her elbows, readying herself for some juicy gossip.

'It's Mack ... ever since he bought his farm, he's been asking if I've heard from you and if you are coming down to Glenorchy again.' Hope started to gather up their picnic plates and utensils and wrapped them in a tea towel while Jessie sat all ears with her mouth wide open waiting to hear the rest of the surprising news.

'And the other day he was saying how lonely it is on the farm.'

Jessie didn't know what to say. What was Hope getting at?

'It's pretty lonely I guess living in a large barn on his own. He has been slowly renovating it, trying to do it himself mostly, and sometimes with help from men at church.' Hope kept watching Jessie's face, looking for her reaction.

'Come on, let's get going. I have to get back and phone my new intake of riding students who are arriving next week.'

Jessie was quiet during the ride back and the girls let the horses have long reins as they made their way back to the ranch just before dusk.

***

Friday came soon enough and Jessie just moped around the stables feeding the foals and mucking out. She started thinking about what direction her life would take if they rejected her application. The breakfast cereal she had wolfed down had risen to the top of her throat and that sick feeling had returned. She'd forgotten to bring her antacid tablets to the ranch.

'Jessie! Are you there? Can you hear me? There's a phone call for you ... it's Max.' Cole poked his head through the stable doorway.

She swallowed the lump in her gullet, placed the pellet bucket back on the shelf, and rushed out the door.

'Thanks, Cole,' she yelled after him. 'Tell him I'm coming.'

Cole went back into the ranch house with Jessie in tow.

'Hope you don't mind me taking the call. They are often for me about my equine breeding program.' He handed her the phone. The voice on the other end did not sound like Max. He was a lot more serious than the jovial fellow who interviewed her—this time his voice sounded flat.

'I'm sorry, Jessie but we've met with a few obstacles regarding your job application,' he stammered.

Her heart sank and her throat tightened.

'The thing is ... the panel of people who screened your credentials needed to vote for or against your application and it was fifty-fifty. They were all men and half of them did not agree to have a female as the local rural vet for this area. In fact, we seldom see female vets in these parts. I'm sorry, Jessie as I think you are tops.'

'Oh, so what does this mean? I haven't been successful then?' She squeezed back the tears that were threatening to sting her eyes and wiped them away with her hand.

'I don't mean that at all. The Board have accepted your application, thanks to Joel and Cole. They sent strong supportive letters as part of your references. The farmers in this area highly respect these men and the directors could not refuse you on this basis. Of course, the Board had my endorsement as well. It's just that you may get a bit of a hard time from those who had rejected your application, but you just have to stand your ground. Joel and Cole will back you up.'

Jessie's voice quavered. 'What do I do next then?'

'I'll be around tomorrow with your contract. All the directors get one as well. I'll be staying on and working with you for a while before I hand the practice over to you. I'll see you in the morning.'

Jessie couldn't stop thanking him. But most of all she gave thanks to God for standing in the gap for her.

***

That evening, after she'd phoned Peter Cranston to let him know her decision to leave and take up the role of Glenorchy's remote vet, Hope and Cole made a celebration dinner for her. Cole was eager to get her involved in his breeding program with the horses and couldn't stop talking about it. He would require Jessie to certify the mares suitable for reproduction. At last, she was at home in the high country—her dream was about to come true.

Chapter Four

A month had gone by since Jessie's holiday on Dart River Ranch. She'd been flat out winding up her business with the clinic in the Waikato and organising a place to live in Glenorchy. Fortunately one of Hope's church parishioners had come to the rescue. A farmer and his wife had a cottage to rent not far from Dart River Ranch. Jessie had few belongings in the small studio she'd rented near the clinic, so moving was simple.

'Not long now ...we'll be sorry to see you go, I have to say.' Peter Cranston's voice was breaking up. 'I don't blame you though, at your age. You remind me of when I was a young vet. Life was one great adventure, and no one was going to hold me back. You give it your best and I'll be watching the space to see where you end up.'

Jessie avoided his gaze. Peter Cranston had been good to her—a great mentor. She was indebted to him.

'I'll be back up this way to see you all. I have friends in the area, remember?'

The last few weeks flew by and before she knew it, she was back on the Air New Zealand DC-10 flight to Queenstown. She had her belongings sent down by the truck before she arrived.

***

The first night in Glenorchy, she stayed at Dart River Ranch and Hope collected her from the airport. The two girls sat up late discussing their plans for the next day.

19

'I'm going to take you to your new home tomorrow. Lance and Mary, your new landlords will be there to meet you at ten. I'll help you unpack as your packages all arrived here yesterday.'

'Oh, you don't have to go to all that trouble. I have all week and you're busy running your riding classes.'

'No, I haven't any groups for a while. They start again in a few weeks.' Hope sat flipping through the pages of her diary.

'I'm not expected to accompany Max on his rounds until next Monday.' Jessie pulled out the hair tie from her ponytail and refastened it.

'That's good because I have a mare about to foal and I thought you could assist her,' said Cole.

'Don't pressurise her. She may not be ready for that yet.'

'Yes, I am. I can't wait. Even though I've helped Dad with calving for years and did some hands-on during my training, I've never done it unassisted before.'

That night, Jessie tossed and turned, struggling to get to sleep after all the excitement. She couldn't wait to be in her new home and going off visiting farms each day. Hope's father had loaned her an old Ute that was still drivable, although it made all sorts of grunts and gurgles. She had planned to buy a vehicle once she had started work.

The next morning, feeling energised in spite of getting off to sleep late, Jessie was eager to get to her cottage. Joel's boisterous border collie almost knocked her over as he greeted her.

She wandered outside looking for Hope and Cole. They'd already started feeding the animals and checking on the broodmares in the stables. She inhaled deeply, filling her lungs with the clean mountain air. The early morning sun warmed her soul.

'Hi, Jessie. I wasn't sure if you wanted to sleep in so I didn't wake you. We're going in for breakfast now. My folks have already left to visit my Aunt in Geraldine.'

Jessie was ravenous after all the travelling and intensity of the previous day. There was plenty of food on the table so she didn't go hungry.

'How about you get all your stuff unpacked at the cottage and come back here when we think that mare is about to foal. Unless she has it overnight. When she's close, we'll let you know,' said Hope.

'Sure, sounds good to me. I'm only ten minutes away.'

'By the way ... Do you remember the young black stallion that was sired by one of the horses in Dad's first muster? He's a three-year-old, stunning Arab. Mack purchased him from my father and has named him, Zoro. He wants to show him as well as use him for as a workhorse on the farm. For a young stallion, he possesses a mellow nature.'

'Oh, really. I'd like to see him sometime... the horse, I mean.'

Cole looked sideways at Hope and chuckled.

'Sure thing, Jessie. I'm sure I can arrange that sometime,' said Cole with a grin.

The girls cleared the table while Cole went back outside.

'Come on. Let's get your things over to the cottage. We can pack both vehicles up. I'll take our Chevy and you can follow me as I know the way.'

Soon after they arrived at the cottage, Jessie's landlords turned up. They presented Jessie with a bunch of multi-coloured hydrangea flowers by Mary who took a large vase out of the laundry cupboard.

'Here—I remembered the last tenants left it and don't want it back. Flowers will help to give the cottage a homely feeling,' said Mary.

Instantly Jessie took a liking to her new landlady.

'And you are our new vet? That will make a change having an attractive young girl instead of a worn-out old codger like Max,' said Lance.

'Hey, cut it out!' Mary elbowed him hard and they both laughed. At least Jessie knew that some people were on her side.

They showed her around the cottage and how everything worked. 'Don't hesitate to ring us if you need anything.'

Hope poked her head in the bathroom. 'Oh, good, a shower.'

'The water pressure is a bit weak but I'm getting someone in to move the hot water cylinder which will fix that. One of us could visit you each week to collect the rent. Hope says you'll be worshipping at our church in Glenorchy. Is that right?' Lance walked back outside, inspecting the water tank on his way out. Jessie followed.

'Yes, I will actually.'

'Well, why don't you just hand me a cheque at church at the end of each week instead. That'll keep you on the straight and narrow now, won't it?'

Jessie begrudged being obligated to attend church so they could collect the rent. She was reluctant to have them come to the cottage every week as though they were checking up on her. Being a modern, independent woman this didn't go down well.

'I'd rather set up an automatic payment at my bank. That way you can guarantee to get your money on time.'

Mary and Lance looked at each other, shrugged. 'I suppose that's your decision,' said Lance, and then driving off.

Hope helped Jessie to unpack.

'Let's get started. With the two of us doing it, we'll have it finished in no time,' said Hope tearing the duct tape off the first box.

***

Her first night in the cottage took Jessie some getting used to. There was a good bed with a firm mattress that Hope's parents had given her. The cotton curtains appealed to her. They were very similar to the ones in her bedroom at her home in Bethlehem— light blue with pink flowers to match the wallpaper.

Jessie's overfatigue caused her to toss and turn. Luckily she was accustomed to all the farm sounds, having grown up being surrounded by noisy cattle and sheep.

Her windows had wire security screens that she locked, but most of all she was never alone. Her relationship with God was stronger than ever and his presence was with her wherever she went. She started to pray to settle her mind—

Surround me with your hedge of protection, God. Bless this house and cleanse it of anything that is not of you. Amen. Finally, her sleep was deep and undisturbed.

***

Jessie woke with sunlight exploding through the crack in her curtains and the phone ringing. She wasn't properly awake as she rolled out of bed to run for the phone and almost fell.

'Morning, Hope. Sorry, I'm not awake yet. I didn't get off to sleep for ages and must have slept in. What's the time?'

'Don't worry ... it's still early ... eight o'clock. Sorry to bother you, but the mare went into labour in the early hours of this morning and she's still going. Do you want to assist?'

'Really? That's wonderful, of course, I do. I'll be there right away.'

'Make sure you have a good breakfast as you'll need it. Max has already checked her when her waters broke and he was happy for you to be there. Dad knows what to do too if you get into trouble.'

Jessie dressed and rushed her breakfast down. She had a good appetite which was usually the case in the mountains.

Driving the Ute was a new experience on the rough, windy road to Dart River Ranch. There was too much play in the steering and she had trouble keeping it steady. The next thing on her agenda will be a new vehicle, that's for sure.

As she drove up to the ranch house, Joel waved out to her by the stables, followed by Hope. She quickly parked her vehicle and rushed up to them.

'Am I too late? Is everything alright?'

'No, you're just in time. It's your turn now.'

Jessie poked her head over the stable door and let herself in. Hope had gone back to the mare and was sitting on the ground rubbing the horse's neck.

'You need to come to this end, Jessie,' Joel said, winking at her. He loved teasing Hope's friends.

The beautiful mare with the shiny black coat kept standing up and lying down on the deep layer of hay.

Before long, the white foetal membrane slowly expelled itself. Joel verbally coaxed Jessie into gently pulling on the two black spindly legs that protruded. Suddenly her heart was in her mouth.

'Remember to breathe, Jessie,' said Joel.

A skinny soft body began to protrude from the mare and as Jessie broke open the membrane, the rest of the foal presented itself. Jessie slipped it out, laying it on the hay next to its mother.

'You've done it! There you are—that wasn't too bad, was it?' Joel patted Jessie on the shoulder. 'You did it all by yourself!'

Jessie was so overcome by it all that she threw her arms around Hope.

'Congratulations!' Hope blurted.

'I'll go inside and give Max a call and tell him you don't need any orientation from him. You're a champion,' Joel said to Jessie, who followed him into the house as they left the mare to bond with her foal. Cole had just arrived from visiting a client and couldn't believe his ears when they said that Jessie had delivered the foal. He'd wanted to be back in time. 'Well, what is it—or is it genderless?' He grabbed a bottle of ginger beer from the fridge. 'Anyone else wants a drink?' He handed the bottles around.

'We have another colt. A black one to replace the foal that has gone to Mack,' said Joel.

'When do you start working with Max, Jessie?' Hope popped the top of her bottle.

'Tomorrow—ah no, sorry, I mean on Monday. He's taking me on farm visits straight away. We don't have a clinic out here. With remote rural vets, it's all home consultations and after-hours they have to take smaller animals into Queenstown. I'll still go to the farms for the large animals, as it's part of my job as a remote vet. I'm not too keen on driving after dark but that's just one of the drawbacks of being a rural vet on call.'

'Wow, good on you. I'm sure you're going to do well out here.'

'Max says we're off to a farm to help with calving and later in the week lambing.'

'Well, that's no problem for you after today's session. You're an expert now.' Hope gave her a warm smile and Jessie lapped up the encouragement.

After she washed up, she headed out to her vehicle.

'I'd best be getting back home. I've still got unpacking to do and I'm pretty tired out. Need to be fresh for Monday. I'll be moving the rest of my stuff in tomorrow.'

'You won't stay for dinner then?' Hope asked.

'That's kind of you, but I'm bushed. I'll call you tomorrow and let you know how I'm going.'

Hope and Cole waved her off as the Ute gave a cough and chugged its way down the driveway. Jessie arrived home and threw off her leather boots. Heading straight for her bed, she collapsed on it, forgetting to remove her Stetson, almost crushing it. After tossing it onto the armchair next to the bed, she relaxed and closed her eyes. Tired more than hungry, she soon fell asleep. When she stirred, it was dark and the cold night air woke her. She hurried outside to secure the Ute and then locked herself in the house. She now had some energy to get herself a meal. If only she didn't have to cook for herself tonight. There was a Chinese food outlet at the end of her street in the Waikato where she could pick up a nutritious meal when she didn't want to cook. Now she would just have to adjust. The nearest grocer, the General Store was a few miles away in Glenorchy and had a limited supply of groceries, so she reckoned on having to stock up once a fortnight in Queenstown.

'Ah!' She remembered she'd taken out a Shepherd's Pie from the freezer—one of the meals that Hope had given her to tide her over until she got on her feet. There were other meals donated to her by her church parishioners that she had frozen too.

Once the meal had been heated up in the oven, she took the enamel dish out and could barely wait to scoop the contents onto a plate. She was so hungry—she smothered it in tomato sauce and sat at the table bolting the food down as if she'd been on a starvation diet.

In the fridge, she saw some of Myra's home-made yoghurt and gulped it down. She was thinking she should start putting her things away into the cupboards and drawers but she'd had enough for the day.

Hope had told her that there was no television reception in the area, only closer to Queenstown which was a disappointment as she had brought a small TV with her. Perhaps she should have rented something closer to all the amenities. But then she couldn't have it both ways—everything at her finger-tips such as peace and tranquillity. That's what she wanted, and she had right there.

Chapter Five

Monday couldn't come fast enough for Jessie. Max was at her gate right on the dot of nine as she expected. She jumped in beside him in his green, 1973 model, four-wheel-drive Land Rover that stank of dog. She held a piece of toast in her hand, licking the sticky jam from her fingers after she crunched into it.

'We've got a bit of a drive this morning up into those hills way up there. I hope you don't get carsick—it's a rough trip, in fact, most of the roads around here are pretty bad. We have to do plenty of driving in this job so you'd better have a decent vehicle.'

'No, I'll be fine. Back home in Bethlehem, the roads are mostly loose metal, so I'm used to it. As soon as I can, I'm going to buy myself a Land Rover like yours that I can sleep in when I get late-night call-outs.'

'Mmm, I'll have a think about that. There may be one going for sale locally. Now ... my first stop is old Ted Gregory's cattle station. We have to drive through Dart Valley near Mount Alfred. Lovely views on the way. You'll get a chance to assist him with calving.'

'Great, that's what I've been looking forward to.'

'Good, you are wearing the right gear. Did you bring a change of clothes? It can get pretty messy.'

'Oh, I know that. I've helped my Dad do it from an early age. I have them in the rucksack you threw in the back.'

Jessie wasn't normally carsick but the way Max swerved around the corners in his Land Rover caused the scrambled egg which she'd eaten earlier rise to her throat and back again.

'What do you think of the countryside around here? It's unique, isn't it?' Max sat tall in his seat, gloating.

'That's why I wanted to be down here. It sure is amazing scenery and the mountain air is so clean.'

The vehicle wound its way up to a cattle station that had spectacular views of Mount Alfred.

'Here we are—time to do some work. Roll up your sleeves my girl.'

Jessie was rearing to go. She grabbed her rucksack and followed Max along a broken path that led to the homestead. Ted must have heard the truck, as he was waiting out on the porch in tan corduroy trousers and Swanndri.

'Gidday, mate,' he said to Max. 'You'll be needing something warm up here.' He glanced at Jessie. 'So you're our new vet. Hope you can cope with the work. You need a bit of muscle for this slog, doesn't she Max?'

'I've got a jacket in this bag, and I'm used to cattle. My father runs beef and sheep.'

'Good. At least you're not just a townie.' Ted smirked.

Jessie found his attitude condescending and not welcoming.

'The cows are out the back. I have my motorbike and you can both fit on that old quad bike.'

'Don't worry Missy, I can drive one of these okay,' said Max, humouring her.

The two of them followed Ted to a paddock not far from the house. He had moved the pregnant cows closer to the homestead, so he didn't have far to go to check on them.

Max carried a large leather bag and Tom had a rope and a few things in a sack.

'She's been going for a few hours and I think this one is breech.' Ted patted the cow on the neck.

'Oh, she has horns! And all that wool. I haven't seen a breed like this before. My Dad just had Friesians.'

'These are Highlanders. You have to watch those horns.' Max took the calving rope off Ted and pulled on a pair of long rubber gloves. 'Here, Jessie. You'll need these. Remember—stay behind her unless you want to become skewered.'

Max began to examine the cow. 'Sure is breech, but one foot is already protruding.' He took Jessie's hand and guided her arm in to grab hold of the legs. They needed to use the calving rope and there was a lot of tugging and waiting until finally, the calf dropped to the ground. It wasn't breathing at first. Max picked it up and dangled it over the gate to clear its airway. Instantly it perked up. Jessie was impressed.

'I've never seen Dad do that before. He used to throw cold water over their heads to stimulate them.'

'Well, I have to teach you something as you're going to be following in my footsteps. I can't muck that up, can I?'

They took off back to the house. Ted thanked them both and invited them in for some refreshments. He offered some cold beer.

'You know me, Ted—I don't drink and drive and Jessie here doesn't drink alcohol. Perhaps you have some cold water?'

'I've something better than that. Some of my wife's home-made lemonade with mint. She's gone into town to get the groceries.'

Jessie's arms were still shaking after all the pulling and straining. She wondered how she would have coped with that situation on her own. They both gulped the beverages down in a hurry.

'We'd better get off. Call us if you have any others in trouble, Ted. We'll find our own way out.'

Jessie's knees were still knocking together as she followed Max back down the path to the Land Rover.

She went quiet on the trip back to Glenorchy, wondering whether she really had jumped in at the deep end. There were few women vets doing this kind of work. Did she have what it takes to survive? She prayed silently for courage. It didn't really take so much strength as technique, those difficult births. Other women do it, so can she?

'You're very quiet all of a sudden. You couldn't stop talking on the way up here, girl. Are you okay?'

'Oh, I'm fine. I guess I was nervous on the way to Ted's or apprehensive more like it. I just didn't know what to expect.'

'You did well up there. You've got nothing to worry about. You knew what you were doing. You'll get into the swing of it and the farmer's do most of it, anyway.'

Jessie trusted Max and was secure in the knowledge that he wouldn't have said that if he had not meant it.

'Lambing isn't so difficult. The animals give birth on their own. It's just when they have difficult labour that we intervene. Down in the Rees Valley, there's a ewe with twins and she needs help right now. The farmer radioed me back at Ted's house—oh yes I must show you how to use my car radiophone before I leave.'

When they entered the valley, Jessie kept scanning the hills to see if she could see any of the wild horses that still remained there. As they turned a bend in the road, a chestnut Kaimanawa horse and foal stood under the trees.

'That's one of the horses from the beech forest—you know the ones that had escaped from that mad Captain.'

'You mean from that rogue, Richardson. He's back in the province, I heard. Apparently, he's trying to start up a horse ranch again near Closeburn. I've heard he has some dubious characters working for him.'

'As long as he keeps down there away from us, I don't mind.'

'We'll have to wait and see if they're trouble or not.'

The welcome Jessie received from the farmer with the ewe giving birth to twins was much warmer than the cool reception from Ted. Joe and his wife offered them afternoon tea which was a treat as they'd eaten their sandwiches earlier without a hot drink. The couple sat asking Jessie a myriad of questions before leading her and Max out to the yard where the ewe was in labour.

'She has just started straining, but the sack hasn't appeared yet.' Farmer Joe let Max take over from this point. The seasoned vet took a look at her. 'She's nearly ready. I can feel the sack just sitting there.'

Within minutes the ewe gave a sigh and one foot started to show, and then the second one. After thirty minutes the head and rest of the body made an appearance. Joe presented the lamb to its mother for her to lick it clean while Max prodded Jessie to assist the next delivery.

'Wait on, we've got another one coming, rear legs first. It's a breech birth. Oh well, good practice for you Jessie. Come and kneel here.'

The ewe was already lying down. Max guided Jessie's hands, and it required some pulling but nothing like the efforts needed with the Highland cow.

Within another half hour, the ewe was busy licking both lambs.

Joe showed Max and Jessie to the laundry where they could wash up. They declined his wife's invitation to go back inside the house afterwards.

As Max drove back out onto the main road, he kept looking at Jessie. 'Are you okay? You look a bit pale.'

'I'm okay, honest. I'm just adjusting to a different bed and I've been doing a lot of unpacking in the last few days.'

'You haven't really had much time to adjust with such a big move and starting work so quickly. Don't worry I won't work you too hard.'

Jessie gave him a half-smile.

'I'm really impressed with your skills. I think you could have handled it all today without my help. Just remember the farmers have experience too, so you're not alone.'

Jessie was wondering if she'd bitten off more than she could chew but she found Max's kind words reassuring.

'I suppose it'll take me a while to get into the swing of things.'

Max dropped her at her gate.

'Coming in for a brew? I'm dying for a cup of tea.'

'No thanks, Jessie. I've got a few urgent calls to make back at the house and I promised Clara I'd put up a shelf for her today.'

'Okay. What have you lined up for tomorrow?'

'I've got a bit of surgery to do near Queenstown in Closeburn. A colleague, Robbie Byrnes from the Vet's Cooperative shares his clinic with me for minor surgical procedures.'

'Oh, great! I love surgery.'

'I want you to come and see what he does, as he'll be a great resource for you. He runs the clinic in Closeburn twice a week. You'll be able to run your own clinic once a week as I have been doing. I'll see you here at eight. I need to get there on time. He has some sterilisations to do and you can assist us.'

When Max drove off, Jessie had butterflies in her stomach that she usually experienced when she didn't know if she was afraid or just excited. Now things were happening. Today she assisted the birth of a Highlander calf and twin Merino lambs. Tomorrow she'll be doing surgery. Did this mean that she was going to cope with this formidable role of the remote vet after all? She hoped it was the forerunner of ongoing success.

***

At the end of the month, Max completed assisting Jessie with her orientation and departed. This was the last she would see of him for a while as he and Clara were about to embark on a trip around the North Island for a few months. Max reassured her she could call him at any time on her radiophone. Robbie Byrnes, the vet she visited near Closeburn would also be at her disposal.

Max had been generous enough to offer her his vehicle while they were away. He said he and his wife would drop it off in the morning before they leave for their trip.

'We'll slip the keys through your cat door.' Before he drove off, he said he was leaving her to it, that she was highly capable, and he had complete confidence in her. He and his wife live in Glenorchy so he would be able to rescue her if she got out of her depth after he returned from his holiday.

'Wait—I forgot something. I'm going to leave you my Motorola Carphone with battery recharger and batteries. I'll give you a quick lesson first. Unless you already know how to use one?'

'Oh, no I don't. I'd been thinking about purchasing one when I go into Queenstown next.'

'Well, you won't have to for a while. Hold on to it and give it back once you've got one of your own. Now let me show you how to use it.' He went into great detail about the channels and ranges of the Carphone. As he started the engine of the Land Rover, he leaned out the window. 'And remember I said to keep the batteries topped up.' He tooted a few times then disappeared out the gate and around the corner out of sight.

Now she was on her own. She was it. The only remote vet for miles. It gave her a foreboding feeling that she kept fighting. At times like this, she prayed for protection, courage, and strength.

***

A month later she had completely settled into her new role and most of the clients so far had been warm and welcoming except for the few grumpy farmers who ruffled her feathers. She was sure she would be able to rise above their prejudice.

Today was her first day off in a long stretch. She had planned to go for a ride on her bicycle in the countryside. She could have gone for a horse ride as Hope had told her she could take Misty out riding any time she liked. But she would rather have her own horse to ride. She intended to buy one, but she told herself the new vehicle must come first.

She pulled her bike out from between all the empty cartons she had thrown into the garage and checked the tyres. Where had she put the bike pump? It was one thing after another that she couldn't find. She'd been so fatigued the first day she was unpacking that she'd just randomly put things away without any kind of system.

She found the pump in her bedside table drawer for some reason. Now, where was her water bottle she took with her on her bike? The one that fits into the bottle holder. She found it crammed into the bottom of her rucksack in her wardrobe.

She was finally ready to go and started to push her bike out the garage door when she heard the phone ring inside the house. She guessed it was Hope and just got to the phone in time, puffing. She was able to say breathlessly, 'Hi Hope. You caught me just in time. I was on my way out on a bike ride.'

'Mack and Cole have organised a hike through the beech forest on Mount Alfred. There are awesome views from up there. I know what an avid climber you are, and when I told Mack that, he insisted you join us.'

'Oh, did he now? I haven't climbed since my school days when Dad used to take my brother and me up Mount Ruapehu. I haven't even got any climbing gear down here.'

'We have all the gear. It can be a bit cold in May but we'll be okay if we have the right clothing. I'll give you some crampons, as you'll need to carry them in your daypack as there is a bit of ice around.'

Jessie guessed she could give it a try as she had missed the mountains when she was in the Waikato, but lately, there had been no time for recreation.

'Drop by at nine on Saturday. You can come with us. Mack says he will meet us at the car park. Why don't you come over for dinner tomorrow night, Jessie? I haven't seen anything of you for a while. Let's celebrate your new role.'

Jessie accepted Hope's invitation the next evening. Once she had eaten a full roast chicken dinner with all the trimmings, she almost fell asleep in the armchair where she sat by the fire in the lounge. The mature low-alcohol apple cider that Cole had uncorked to have with their meal didn't help. It still packed a punch, even without much alcohol and just a small glass with her food was enough to put her to sleep.

'Are you sure you can drive home, Jessie? You can stay in the guest room. I can give you some nightwear.'

'No thanks, I need to do some paperwork before I go to bed. The cool night air will soon wake me up. I'll see you at your house at around nine on Saturday.'

'Wait! I'll just go and get the crampons.' Hope hurried away and brought back the crampons and a thick Anorak.

'Here—you're going to need the jacket as well.'

***

Jessie wound down her window as she pulled out onto the road and took a deep breath of the pure country air. She could smell the newly cut hay in the fields opposite and caught a whiff of fresh silage that gave her a nostalgic feeling reminding her of home.

The full moon lit up the road like a city highway and illuminated the terrified opossums that stood still on the road, dazzled by the headlights of her vehicle. Jessie was aware of them and drove with extra caution at night. She hated seeing animals that had been killed on the road by passing vehicles, even though this was sometimes unavoidable.

She had to force herself to stay awake to do her book work. Now that she was working freelance, she had to complete a report of all her visits at the end of each month for the Vet Cooperative. It was going to be a lot of work for her keeping on top of tax returns and such like. But it would all be worth it in the end. Who knows? Maybe one day she could afford to pay an assistant to deal with that.

Early the next morning her first visit was to a small Hereford Stud near the Rees River. The farmer, Buck, was a widower, one of the grumpy men that Max talked about who didn't like female vets. Some of his cattle needed, health checks, as there had been an outbreak of Leptospirosis in the Canterbury area and due to the recent flooding of his farm, he was worried a few of his herd had contracted it. He had phoned the Vet Cooperative to request a visit but didn't know the vet would be Jessie.

She knocked on the door loudly but still, there was no answer. She then tried the large cast-iron knocker. No one came to the door.

'Who are you? What are you wanting?'

Jessie nearly jumped out of her leather boots as she turned around to see a cantankerous figure standing over her in his threadbare denim dungarees.

'Oh ... hi. I'm Jessie your new vet.'

'What did you say? Where's Max? He usually comes up here.'

Jessie shook inside. This man was one of the difficult farmers Max had warned her about.

'Sorry, didn't you know? Max has retired and is now away on holiday. He has handed his clients over to me. I am a senior vet.'

'Oh, is that right? Well, I don't agree with all these changes and I don't know if you can handle the cattle.'

'That's not a problem—I grew up on beef and sheep farm. Let me have a look at them.'

'Well, I'm not happy about all this, but I suppose I've got no jolly choice! Follow me then.'

Jessie picked up her leather bag and traipsed along behind him to a large barn where he kept half a dozen heifers inside away from the others. She pulled some rubber gloves out of her bag and other equipment then started examining each animal while Buck held them still. When she'd finished examining them and writing her report, Buck invited her into the house for a cup of tea and offered her a seat in the dining room.

'If you were a bloke, I'd offer you a cold beer.'

'Actually, I don't drink alcohol—I don't like it. I prefer tea, thanks.'

'Hmm. I'll put the kettle on.'

Jessie's awkwardness caused her continual chatter. 'I don't think your cattle have Leptospirosis. It appears to be some kind of cold virus. It would be best to keep them away from the others, especially the one with a cough. Perhaps let them bed in your nice warm barn.'

Buck nodded and handed her a plain arrowroot biscuit. She didn't care much for them but accepted.

'Here is my invoice. You can pay by cheque now or post it to me.'

Buck was taken aback by her self-confident assertiveness. 'Right you are. Just wait—I'll go get my book.'

Jessie's eyes darted over to the photos on his fireplace shelf. It looked like his wife and family.

'Have you been on your own long up here?' Jessie dared ask, handing him the invoice.

'Fifty years we lived up here until my wife had a stroke and passed away five years ago. Not much chop on your own. The kids all live overseas.'

Jessie realised why the widowed man would feel bitter. His coldness towards her was not personal at all—just born out of constant loneliness.

***

Some days later Jessie received a late-night call from Hope. She had rung to tell her someone had stolen the young black stallion that Mack had purchased from Joel. That put the damper on her living alone now that she was aware there were criminals in the area.

A few days later she read in the newspaper that the police had no other reporting of stolen horses. The culprits seemed only to have been interested in Mack's new stallion. But why?

The next day Jessie had the day free and popped in to visit Hope who'd done some baking and invited Jessie to stay for afternoon tea.

Jessie stood on the front doorstep struggling to pull her long boots off. 'I'm sure my feet swell up in the heat. I'll have to sit down to get them off.'

'Come in and have a scone. I made some jam with those strawberries I froze last summer.'

'Delicious. I wish I could make scones like yours. Mine come out like rocks.'

'There's a trick to making them. I'll show you on your next day off if you like.'

'So ... what's happened? You know—to poor Mack's stallion.'

'Apparently, they cut the fence to take Zoro out from the back of his farm where there is a small lane they must have used. Mack was distraught since he had seen blood on the grass by the barbed wire fence. The police believe the horse has been targeted and they must have known it was on the property.'

'How would they know? I suppose one of their friends tipped them off. I wonder why they want him that much, to go to such lengths.'

'At least he still has our branding. He has the mark we freeze branded him with. It has DRR for Dart River Ranch on his rump just by his tail. We photograph all our horses' brandings so we have a record of it,' said Hope.

'Keep me informed. I'll make enquiries with all my clients and keep an eye out on their properties too.'

***

Saturday couldn't come quick enough for Jessie. She'd been up early, full of anticipation for the climb up Mount Alfred. She packed her truck and headed off to meet up with Hope and Cole who were outside in the driveway packing their Ute already.

'Just in time for a brew before we head off. Sling your backpack into the back of the Ute.' Cole walked over to help her.

Jessie glanced over at Hope and for the first time could detect she was actually pregnant although her slight build seemed to make it not so noticeable. 'Are you sure you should be hiking in your condition? It's not exactly a walk in the park, is it? I hope you have checked with your midwife.' Jessie put her hand on Hope's shoulder to make sure she had her attention.

'Don't worry, I'm fine. Yes, I've checked with my midwife. I'm four months now, and it's okay as I did a few strenuous hikes before I got pregnant. I'm quite fit.'

'Okay, you win. Please be careful.'

39

They drank their tea while Cole checked the petrol and oil in the Ute.

'Come on, ladies, time to go or Mack will be standing in the car park on his own.' Cole threw the last bag into the Ute.

As they wound their way up through Dart River Valley along the Glenorchy-Routeburn Road, Jessie caught sight of patches of snow on the branches of trees and as they climbed higher up the valley, ice appeared on the road.

'Darn! I heard there had been a bit of snow falling last night but not this low. I hope we won't need chains on the tyres.' Cole leaned out his window to inspect the road.

'Oh ... how are we going to get to the summit if there's snow?'

'You'll be okay. We are carrying all the right gear. It's not a huge mountain, in fact, it's one of the smaller ones.' Cole looked at Jessie in the back seat. She just sat still. Was she quietly regretting she had agreed to come?

'If I can do it in my state, you can Jessie. We can take our time. The sign up there says it takes six to eight hours, but that's there and back. There's no rush, we have all day.'

Mack was sitting on a log eating an apple. His face was much bronzer since Jessie saw him last and he had gained solid muscle. Perhaps he had just grown up. She almost tripped when she stepped out of her vehicle.

'Can I help with anything?' he asked her as she went to the back of the Land Rover to fetch her bag.

'No, I've got it covered thanks.'

'It's been a while since I saw you last. At their wedding, wasn't it?' Mack pointed at Hope and Cole.

'Yeah, I guess so. Golly, it's been that long.'

'I thought you would have been down sooner as you used to like it here so much.' Mack was persistent.

'I would have been down, but the clinic was always so busy and short-staffed. I just couldn't get away.'

'Well, she's here now, Mack so let's make the most of it,' replied Hope, who appeared irritated by his seeming annoyance that Jessie hadn't been around.

'Shall we get going then? I don't know what to expect up there seeing that it snowed up here last night. We'll just have to be careful. Hope—you take a break whenever you want and we'll stop.' Cole was the gentleman, Jessie thought as she imagined what it would be like to have such a kind, caring man in her life. But for now, she'd have to take care of herself. She was even wondering if she could keep up with Hope, even though she was pregnant.

Chapter Six

They walked slowly, stumbling over the large roots and vines that covered the forest pathway, zigzagging their way up towards the summit. The fresh snow became thicker and icicles appeared on the branches of the beech trees.

Two hours later on the last lap to the top, as they rounded the corner past huge overhanging rocks, a carpet of snow covered the track. A thick mist hung over the whole area giving it a mystical appearance then it quickly disappeared, revealing a bright blue sky that illuminated the white snow.

'Let's stop for lunch. I've packed a thermos of hot chocolate if anyone would like to have some.' Hope pulled it out and placed it on a lightweight rug she had packed to sit on.

They sat eating and talking. Mainly it was Mack asking Jessie all about her work in the clinic in Waikato and her new role in Glenorchy. His eyes stayed fixated on her.

'We need to prepare ourselves if we are going any further as the mountain can be prone to freak blizzards. There was one up here last night. There's usually not so much snow around this early in the year. We'll need to get our crampons on now as I can see ice on the rocks and it's pretty steep going up there. I'm carrying some ropes just in case,' said Cole.

'I've packed some climbing ropes too,' Mack added.

Jessie stopped eating and started fumbling around in her backpack. Her face dropped and furrows appeared in her brow.

'What's wrong Jessie? Is everything okay?'

'Ah, no. I think I've forgotten something and you're not going to be very happy.'

Mack stared at her, squinting through the glare from the snow.

'I've left my crampons behind—the ones you lent me, Hope.'

'Oh no! You won't be able to go up to the summit now. I'll have to stay back with you and let the men go up without us,' said Hope.

'No, she can't continue the climb now. We'll have to turn around and walk back down,' said Cole, gruffly.

'You won't have to do that. I'm wearing special tramping boots for icy terrain. They grip really well. I'll be perfectly fine, don't worry.'

Hope looked over at Mack who was the most experienced climber amongst them. 'What do you think, Mack? Should she continue with all that ice up there?'

'No. I think it would be foolish, but Jessie will have to make up her own mind. Tell you what—I'll accompany Jessie on the steep incline towards the summit and it would be a good idea if Hope sticks close to Cole. What do you all think?'

Cole looked at the two girls and nodded. 'He's right, girls. We need to go in twos from now on and tread very carefully.'

The hike up the last stretch of the mountain was arduous. Hope needed to have several breaks to catch her breath and Jessie began to think it was a bad idea all around for Hope to be taking such a risk. But she was just as experienced a climber as Jessie was and Cole was overprotective. But it was herself she should have been more concerned about and she was about to find out very quickly.

The terrain had changed suddenly from thick, crisp snow to ice and now and then Jessie's boots slipped but she managed to keep her balance. 'Here, take my arm if you think you are slipping,' Mack said, as he stopped momentarily.

'Oh, that won't be necessary—I'm fine. You don't need to fuss.'

Within minutes after saying that, her body began sliding away from Mack's side uncontrollably. Her boots suddenly acted like skis and shot sideways propelling her towards the side of the narrow mountainside where she thought she was going to plummet over the edge. Before she realised what had happened, she jettisoned onto her side causing a stabbing pain in her shoulder. Her body continued to jettison itself then bang—instantly it reached its destination with a hard thud as her back slammed against an ice wall—she had fallen in a deep crevice. The echo of Hope screaming in the distance penetrated her ears.

Her ribs hurt. She had the wind knocked out of her. Worst of all, she peered downwards and all she could see was a blue abyss. As she stayed dead still, she could hear Mack calling from up above.

'Don't move Jessie, just don't move. I'm coming down to get you,' he yelled. Jessie detected a quaver in his voice. All she could muster was a faint, 'Okay Mack.'

He tied the rope around his waist and threw it down to her yelling, 'Grab hold of this loop if you can and place it over your head until I get down to you.'

Cole made Hope stay back and sit on a nearby rock that he had scraped the snow off. He carefully walked over to see if he could help.

'I'm going to set up a belay for you to bring her up on after I have abseiled down to her and set up her harness. What do you think?'

Cole inspected the ice. 'Ah, that's pretty solid. Best test it with your weight first, of course.'

Mack poked around until he found what he thought was solid enough ice for the screws and secured the ropes to the anchors.

Jessie waited patiently for him to abseil down to her. A dark cloud of guilt and regret began to descend on her. What has she done? Why was she so stubborn and put all her friends at risk? Mack will think she is so stupid. Her thoughts tormented her while she waited on a narrow ledge. She prayed quietly—*Please God, keep us all safe, and give the men the strength to get us both back up to safety. Thank you.*

Waiting the few minutes for Mack seemed like hours. Then he appeared at her side. She could hardly feel her hands in her sodden woollen gloves. She hadn't thought to bring leather gloves with her. Mack helped her remove them and gave her his spare leather pair.

'I'm sorry, Mack. I had no idea what was initially a fine sunny day would turn out like this. We should have listened to the weather report.'

'The report was for fine weather today. It's just that we thought the freak snowstorm last night was in the higher mountains, not here. Let's get on. I'm going to attach some ropes to you and Cole will belay you back up. You will have to dig your boots in as hard as you can to try to give you some lift. I'll be right beside you with and another rope will attach us.'

Cole managed to get Jessie safely back up top with Mack guiding her all the way up. She collapsed with relief, prostrate on the snow. When she had freed herself from the ropes, the weight of guilt bombarded her again. She stood up then trudged over and sat on the rock next to Hope and Mack followed suit.

'I'm sorry I've caused all this trouble. I didn't realise how dangerous it would be without crampons. I was so determined to see the views from up here I lost perspective and put you all at risk.'

'And I should have insisted that you turn back when you asked me what I thought,' said Mack. 'Let's get going back to where the path is safe. I think we'd better get Hope back down out of this cold.' He looked at her. 'Your poor baby must be cold in your little oven.' With that, Cole came to Hope's rescue and helped her back on the path.

Mack's comments warmed Jessie's soul as he revealed his caring and compassionate nature. She was beginning to have strong feelings for him.

'Thanks, Mack. I appreciate your concern,' said Hope, smiling and patting him on his back.

Mack and Jessie started the descent with Hope and Cole in close pursuit as they cautiously made their way back down the mountain.

When they reached the bush and beech trees, they stopped for a rest and some food.

'I've brought another thermos of hot chocolate. It's in your pack, Cole.' Hope nodded at Cole who had removed his pack.

'Oh, so that's why it was so heavy. Let's get into it then.'

'I've got cups in my pack and some choky biscuits,' she said as she took off her own pack and placed it next to a large rock.

As they enjoyed their hot drinks, Jessie sat on an old log looking quite dejected. Mack must have noticed as he came along and sat next to her, putting his arm across her shoulders.

'Look, girl. Don't dwell on what happened up there. We were all at fault. We should have just turned around and come back down. Don't keep beating up on yourself.'

'Thanks, Mack.'

Hope approached and handed them both the packet of chocolate biscuits.

'I've got a bar of dark chocolate so we can have a decadent chocolate indulgence.' Jessie stood up and grabbed a packet from her backpack. She handed around a large bar of dark, almond nut chocolate.

For the rest of the descent down the mountain, Jessie's legs were like jelly from the rush of adrenaline that had been racing through her body. She noticed that Mack was still walking close by her protectively all the way to the carpark below.

When she arrived at the vehicle, Hope was leaning on the bonnet having a discussion with Cole and looked up as Jessie stood behind her.

'Oh, there you are. Are you okay after all the trauma? Mack said you have sore ribs.'

'Oh, they're alright. Just bruised probably.'

Mack joined them. 'I think she was pretty brave back there. I noticed you were super calm.' He nodded at Jessie. 'There's still the mountain climber in you,' he said with a gleam in his eyes.

Hope stood up and stretched her back then rubbed her abdomen. 'We'd better be getting back. I have a heap of papers to sort out before my riding class starts on Monday. It's the school holidays and I have a group of college children arriving,' said Hope.

'Jessie, why don't you ride with me? I can drop you home.'

'That's nice of you, Mack but I can't—my car is at Hope's house. I came with them.'

Mack's face dropped.

'Oh, okay. Perhaps another time.'

'Yes, that would be great. You could pop over and visit sometime.' Instantly Jessie regretted being so forward and impulsive.

'I'd like that. I'll take you up on it.'

Later that night, just as she was about to drift off to sleep, Jessie had been going over the day's events in her mind. She had relieved herself of the guilt but now she wanted to find some way to make it up to Mack. He was the one who had really risked his own safety by rescuing her. How was she going to make it up to him?

She started to make a plan in her mind about how she could help Mack get Zoro back. Perhaps she could fabricate some kind of reason to visit the farms in the area and offer to give their horses a free health examination to check them for the Equine Influenza. The authorities have already quarantined the cases they found. The outbreak started to spread in the Queenstown area. This was the perfect justification for Jessie to visit farms where there are horses as they are now all at risk of getting the disease.

Chapter Seven

Perhaps there was going to be a breakthrough in her quest to find Zoro. Jessie checked all of Max's patients' records to find out which farms carried horses. A week later the replies started trickling in and she had a positive response, no refusals. They were not able to refuse on legal grounds and if they did, Jessie could obtain a Court order to enter their property if she suspected an animal had an infectious disease, especially if there was an outbreak in the area. She spent another week making appointments over the phone. She had more than a dozen farms to visit locally taking tissue and blood samples and identifying diseases in sick animals.

This placed an extra burden on Jessie. In the meantime, Mack had called to ask if he could drop by as he was heading over her way. Jessie's head was spinning, engulfed by the hefty workload with all the extra visits to make. She turned him down and said she would catch up with him, once she had reduced her workload. She didn't tell him her plan to try to find Zoro—not yet. She wanted to wait until she had some positive results to give him.

After two weeks of checking out every horse on fifteen farms in the area, she came to a stalemate. The day she finished the last visit, she went home early and crashed on her bed, every muscle in her body aching, listening to the pounding of her heart hard against her eardrums. She was thinking her blood pressure must have risen to hear her heart that loudly. Within minutes, her eyes drooped, and she drifted into a deep sleep. Two hours later she awakened to the cold and a fly buzzing around her head. She'd forgotten to take the meat out of the freezer for her evening meal and succumbed to eating leftover lamb curry from the previous day.

After wolfing down her food and washing it down with some of Hope's home-made ginger beer, she stretched out on a lounge chair and perused her list of farms she visited. Not one of them had a horse that slightly resembled Zoro, though she saw plenty of black horses. That was it. She wasn't going to be able to prove to Mack that she wasn't an idiot after all.

***

Jessie received a visit from Cole. He told her that Butch had read in the local news that Captain Richardson had purchased a small farm near Queenstown near Lake Wakatipu and had started a horse ranch there. He had some ranch hands that had been acting suspiciously in the area and local farmers were keeping an eye on them. Cole went on to say that he'd been complaining to folk about the Kaimanawa herd he'd lost in the hills around the Rees Valley several years ago and that some local rancher had captured them and taken possession of them. He was carrying a huge grudge, according to Butch and said he would find them and get his horses back. But that would be illegal. Of course, Jessie asked Cole to let Joel know as soon as possible in case there was any trouble from the ranch hands or Richardson himself as she clearly remembered Max telling her that he thought the ranch hands were thugs.

All this set Jessie thinking and later that day she picked up the phone and called Cole back to suggest Butch do some snooping around Richardson's ranch. She believed it was a possibility they could have taken Zoro if they knew he was from his original herd. Jessie suggested that Butch make some excuse to get onto his farm.

***

49

Butch drove up to the large wooden gate. He could see that Richardson was home as his truck was sitting in the driveway. He walked up to the door, knocked, and peered through a side window to see if there was any movement. No one came to the door. The sound of dogs barking in the field at the back of the farm was evidence that he must have been working them away from the ranch house. Butch wandered over to the stables, hesitated then walked on. In the distance on the far side of the ranch, he caught a glimpse of a tall figure and heard him snarling gruffly at one of the dogs which were busy rounding up a flock of sheep.

Butch walked along through the entrance to the stables and carefully peered into each stall. He had seen four horses but not one of them was black. Zoro wasn't amongst this lot.

He cautiously wandered around the fence line that bordered the ranch house and the paddocks. He scanned each paddock meticulously. In one field there was just a small herd of Jersey heifers. In the next, a couple of bulls and then in the one next to that, to his surprise, more horses. Yes! There was a black one.

As he walked closer to the fence, there he stood, noble-looking—his head held high in the air in such a way it gave him a majestic look, with his tail flying high too. To Butch's amazement, the stallion and two other horses approached him at the fence. Then the other two horses started fighting, rearing, and the black one appeared annoyed, kicking out at them. In a split second, Butch saw it—the letters DRR just below his tail. The other horses galloped off. The young black horse stayed at the fence. When Butch put his hand out, the stallion licked his fingers. 'Well, you're a tame one, aren't you? This isn't your home and we are going to get you out of here.' Butch could see that the horse had a wound, a deep cut that hadn't healed properly and obviously festering.

'Hey! What are you doing here? Clear out!'

Butch swung around to see a tall, unshaven Richardson looming over him. Butch was a strong, stocky fellow but short in stature. He startled, almost falling back against the fence, although he wasn't afraid of him.

'Gidday—Butch Rogers is my name. I'm visiting farms in the area to offer a free hoof check and if you want, I can offer a substantial discount for shoeing for first-time clients.'

'Is that right? What did you say your name is ... Butch, did you say? Oh yeah, I heard you've been the local blacksmith for thirty years. Is that right?'

'Sure is. I suppose you think I'm just drumming up business but I like to have a good rapport with all the locals. I offer the best rates for miles around here.'

'Fair enough. Have you time, today? I'll get those horses into the stalls if you like.'

'Sorry mate. I'll have to book you next week sometime. By the way—I noticed that wound on the young black stallions shoulder. It's infected, mate. You really should get that seen by the vet as the infection can affect the muscle and he could end up lame.'

'Oh, okay. I'll get that seen to. What day can you come next week?'

'How about Friday? I have a whole day free then.'

'Great. I'll see you out that gate—darn thing the latch keeps jamming.'

Butch couldn't believe he actually spoke to the culprit who stole Mack's stallion. Richardson waved him off while Butch was feeling a little guilty that he was about to report him to the police. He couldn't wait to get home to ring Mack and Jessie.

Mack came off the phone to Butch and tried hard to control the large teardrops that oozed from his eyes. It didn't work. With a huge sigh, he let go of the bottled-up tension he'd been harbouring all these weeks of waiting and praying, deeply missing the friendly young stallion to whom he had become so attached. He had spent hours training Zoro so that he became easy to manage and was a fine workhorse for the farm. Wait till he tells Cole.

Once he had composed himself, he rang Cole and asked him to join him and go to the police and then retrieve Zoro and bring him back in his horse truck. He also let Jessie know what they were doing.

The next day, the two men sat at the local police station showing the officers the photos of Zoro's branding and every photo and video clip that Mack had of him. Cole was there as a witness as he had photos of him when newborn and one of him being branded.

The police accompanied the men to Richardson's farm and arrested him for theft while Cole and Mack loaded Zoro into the truck and took him home.

The first thing Mack did when Zoro was in the truck was to phone Jessie. 'Please, can you come, Jessie? I'm really worried that the wound might turn into septicaemia. He should have had antibiotics ages ago.'

'Sure, no problem. I'll be there as soon as I can. I'll just pack my treatment bag and be off.'

At last, Jessie had found a way to return Mack's rescuing gesture by making sure she healed that bad wound on Zoro's shoulder. *Thank you, God. I knew you'd come through for me and find me a way to settle scores with Mack. You know how much this means to me.*

Jessie sang in a high voice all the way to Mack's farm with her windows wide open. A farmer driving past with his truck window wound down called out 'beautiful!' and tooted at her.

For the next few weeks, Jessie visited Zoro every day to observe the result of the antibiotics she had given him. Of course, there was plenty of time for her to get to know Mack really well and a strong friendship began to blossom.

Chapter Eight

Today was Jessie's first proper day off in months. Since she'd taken on the extra task of visiting Zoro each day to attend his wound, she'd found no time for herself to unwind.

More snow had fallen in the nearby hills and completely covered the mountain tops. She was grateful for the old potbelly stove for burning wood. It stood in the corner of her lounge but it had gone out during the night although the lounge was still warm from the remaining embers. She'd been so tired the night before that she'd forgotten to top the fire up before she went to bed.

She flopped into her lounge armchair and was trying to decide what to do for the rest of the day when she heard banging.

Who would be visiting her, apart from Hope? She hadn't said anything about dropping around to see her. The banging became much louder, so she got out of her chair to check the door. As she stood up, she almost jumped out of her skin. There was a tanned face and leather Stetson filling the frame in her window.

'Mack! I wonder what brings him here,' she muttered on her way to open the door.

'I'm not too early, am I? Happened to be just passing on my way back from the General Store to pick up some hard feed for my sheep. I've had some heavy snow in some of my lower paddocks and they need extra feed.'

'No, it's not too early. I've been awake since dawn. I got a bit cold when the Pot Belly went out. Please ... come on in. I'll put the kettle on.' Jessie stopped at the mirror in the hall to push her hair into place but it was unmanageable. It needed a trim, and she hadn't had the time to go into Glenorchy to the only hairstylist for miles. She appeared dishevelled.

Meanwhile, Mack was struggling to get his boots off and his socks were wet. Jessie glanced at the wet socks. 'Here, bring them by the fire. I'll just stoke it up again. Put them on this rack and they'll be dry by the time we've finished our tea.'

'Actually, the reason I'm here is to ask if you'd like a load of wood. I've heaps of pines on my farm and I can cut some and bring a truckload over if you like. That's in return for all the care you've given Zoro.'

Jessie was uncomfortable with his offer. In her mind, she was no longer in debt to him after caring for his horse. But she needed the wood.

'That's very kind of you but I'll pay you for it.'

'No, I won't have that. Please let me do it, Jessie. It's no trouble, honest. On one condition though—that you make me one of those to die for blackberry pies you gave me to try when you first moved here, remember?'

'I don't have any berries though. They are summer fruit.'

'No, but I have—I collected plenty from up on the farm last summer and froze them. I eat them occasionally with ice cream. It's a pity it's not blackberry season right now. Look ... I promise you I'll take you out berry picking next summer. There's a great spot not far from here.'

'I'll look forward to that when I can get a break. I'll be back in a few minutes—I'll just pour the tea.'

Jessie scurried into her bathroom and quickly brushed her hair. She desperately wanted to change her old worn-out track pants and tee-shirt and put on something more eye-catching but it would be far too obvious and Mack sat waiting patiently for his cup of tea.

She carried the tray of tea, a plate of muffins she had made the night before and tomato sandwiches into the lounge.

'Ah—fresh baking. How do you find time to do all that as a full-time rural vet?'

'Oh, I usually bake a batch of muffins each week to take in the car on my visits. I take a couple of them and some fruit. That gives me enough energy for the day.'

Mack wolfed down a sandwich and took a muffin.

'Mmm, they taste good. Blueberry, my favourite—oh yes, I knew there was something I wanted to tell you.' He took a large bite of his muffin and then took some minutes to clear his mouth. He continued, 'the crook who stole Zoro—that bloke Captain Richardson—he isn't really a captain any longer, though he used to be when he was in the British army. He's one of those pretentious people who like to pull rank as a civilian. Anyway, he's going to Court next week. The police have plenty of evidence to charge him. This will implicate poor Joel as he'll have to give evidence that he branded Zoro and that one of the Kaimanawa horses was a sire. He'd mustered them legally when they were running wild.'

'Wow! That's pretty heavy, isn't it? Poor Joel having to go to Court. Hope doesn't need all that worry about her father when she's about to have a baby. It's due anytime now.'

'It won't be a problem for Joel. He has given the police plenty of evidence and I'm also a witness. I took part in the muster when we captured Zoro's father. It'll be a storm in a teacup and all blow over pretty quickly. Just you wait and see.'

'Hold on, that's my telephone. Sorry, but I'm on call so I'll have to take it.' Jessie handed Mack another muffin then hurried into the small room she'd made into an office. She picked up the phone. It had an exclusive business landline number. Most of the calls came directly from the Vet Cooperative's Call Centre.

'What! Really? Of course, Cole, I'll be right over.' She put the phone down and hastened back into the lounge.

'I'm sorry Mack but I have to rush away. It seems that Hope has gone into labour and the midwife is miles away at another birth. Cole doesn't want to call the rescue helicopter unless they're sure she's in proper labour and he's asked if I could examine her. They know I've delivered babies when I did a short stint as a paramedic.'

'Really? You'd better go then. I'll shift my truck out of the driveway and I'll be letting you know soon when I can bring that load of firewood over to you.' He leaned on the front door post pulling on his knee-high leather boots after having already grabbed his socks from the fireplace.

Meanwhile, Jessie had picked up her black leather medical bag and said goodbye as she raced into her vehicle. She called out through her window, 'I'll phone and let you know the outcome later tonight. Thanks for the offer of the firewood.' She gave him a warm smile and his face just lit up. He lowered his Stetson at her as she drove off while he walked to his truck with a spring in his step and a radiant grin that wouldn't leave his face.

Chapter Nine

Jessie's Land Rover made its way through the light dusting of freshly fallen snow down the long driveway to Dart River Ranch homestead. Cole was waiting for her on the front porch and rushed out to greet her, his eyes seeming to jump out of his head with angst.

'Quickly, come as fast as you can. Her waters have broken!' he bellowed before Jessie has opened the vehicle's door. Cole rushed forward and grabbed her medical bag, almost dragging her up the steps by her arm. She could hear Hope groaning loudly down the hallway. She hurried into the room where she lay sprawled across the bed, her face twisted with furrowed brows as though she was in a torture chamber. Hope burst forth, 'I'm certainly relieved to see you!'

'I'll have to examine you to see how far you are then I can attend to this pain of yours.' With that, Cole left the room.

'Let me know when you have finished,' he called behind him as he shut the door.

Jessie finished her examination and opened the door to let Cole back in.

'Have you been in a warm bath yet like your midwife advised? Heat is a great pain reliever in childbirth. Let's get you into some warm water.'

'Anything to kill this pain!' Hope bellowed.

'Come on,' Jessie said, tugging on Cole's arm. 'You need to fill that lovely claw bath of yours right to the brim.'

'Won't the baby drown in there?' Cole's eyes almost popped out of his head. He started to hyperventilate.

'She's not fully dilated by a long shot. You are going to need to calm down, slow down your breathing so you can help your wife,' Jessie spouted.

Cole helped Hope get into the bath. She slumped into the water and lay there like a beached whale while Jessie popped a rolled-up towel behind her neck. She took a packet of Epsom salts from her pocket and threw some into the bathwater.

'I'm sorry—I can't administer nitrous oxide gas or give you Pethidine injections. I'm only qualified to use these with animals.'

'Her midwife lent her a TENS machine—you know … it sends some kind of electrical impulses to the skin to help with pain relief. But we've forgotten how to use it.' Cole darted back into the bedroom and pulled the machine out of a cupboard while Hope lay in the bath groaning, but not as loudly as when Jessie first arrived.

'Oh, really?' Jessie leaned over to inspect the machine.

'I know exactly how it works. I would have used it in the first place had I known. But the warm water has certainly made a big difference.'

Almost two hours later, Jessie helped Cole get Hope back onto the bed to review her progress again.

'It won't be long now, Hope. Your baby will soon be on its way,' said Jessie, squeezing her hand.

Cole filled her a hot water bottle to hold then as she lay on her side he carried out the massage that he had so often rehearsed at the ante-natal class in Glenorchy.

An hour later, having examined Hope again, Jessie announced that the baby's head was crowning. 'I can just glimpse your baby's head. You're in the second stage of labour.' She called Cole to come back in and repeated it to him. Before long, Hope was screaming and pushing her baby out with each contraction until a strong, healthy baby boy lay across her abdomen after Jessie had cut the umbilical cord. Hope lay motionless with exhaustion, as she had been in labour for some time before Cole had rung Jessie. As she held her newborn close, Cole hovered gently, his long arms around them both.

Myra, Hope's mother had been eagerly waiting around to help. Cole handed the infant to her to wash, dress, and wrap in the shawl that Hope had made for him. His bassinet was all ready. Jessie dealt with the afterbirth and Cole helped to wash his wife with Myra's help.

'Do you have a name for him yet?' Myra asked?

Cole looked at Hope who nodded her approval. 'Bertie—it's a name we both like. I suppose people will think his proper name is Albert, but it's not. It's going to stay as Bertie.'

Myra's face lit up. 'Oh, you've named him after my father!'

It was just a coincidence that Cole chose the same name as her grandfather but Hope said nothing.

'I know he died before you were born so it's nice you have named Bertie after him, even though he was known as Albert, not Bertie.'

Cole winked at Hope and when Myra looked the other way he whispered, 'Leave it, no harm in letting her think that.'

Hope looked around to see Jessie still hovering over baby Bertie, 'I don't know what we would have done without you, Jessie,' said Hope. 'The midwife had intended to be here but she was called out to another emergency birth.' She wiped the beads of perspiration from her forehead with the back of her hand. 'Are you sure you're in the right occupation, as you were marvellous?'

'That comes from delivering all those lambs with Dad during my youth. I've had a good teacher.'

'Thank God you'd done a paramedics course. Or I could have been giving birth to a calf!' Hope managed to laugh as they both cracked up at that image.

'I hope you'll stay and have dinner with us over at our house,' said Myra. 'Cole can probably manage for a while and Hope just wants to sleep.'

'Sure—thank you, I will. I'll just examine Hope again and make sure everything's in order then I'll be right over.'

After she carried out that procedure and helped Hope put her baby on the breast, Jessie made sure Cole was able to cope and left the three of them alone. She was glad of the break, as it had been challenging for her, quite different from delivering four-legged animals and it had certainly boosted her confidence.

Jessie excused herself straight after her meal and couldn't wait to get home to phone Mack with the great news. Or was there perhaps another reason her heart was pounding as she got in the door and picked up the phone to ring him?

***

She struggled to control her breathing when he answered.

'Oh, hello, Mack. You wanted me to let you know the outcome of Hope's labour. She gave birth to a strong, healthy baby boy at four o'clock this afternoon. I stayed there to help clean her up and her parents invited me for dinner. Now I'm bushed—almost as exhausted as Hope is. Oh, by the way, they have named him, Bertie.'

'Wow! I'd say you are some special kind of vet that can do midwife stuff as well as look after animals. Very impressive.' Jessie went quiet. Her cheeks began to burn with embarrassment.

'Well ... catching up on our earlier conversation today. I said to give me a call when you want me to bring the firewood over to you. I hear we're in for a cold winter and we may get some heavy snow around here before too long. You'll need that fire.'

Jessie came off the phone and crashed onto her couch. The fire she'd lit in the morning was still burning as she lay there dozing. She imagined cosy evenings sitting in front of a fire with heavy snow outside with a fat cat lying on the hearth and enjoying a visit from Mack—letting his charming voice lull her into oblivion. She quickly shook herself out of her fantasy putting such idle thoughts out of her mind. Why would he be interested in a woman vet? Any relationship she'd had up until now had never lasted. The men were afraid of commitment. Maybe they just didn't like vets. Would Mack be any different? The men she had met in the

60

Waikato had appeared to be after a dolly bird and she certainly wasn't anything like that. She'd been a bit of a tomboy in her pursuits but she dressed like a lady when she did ever dress up. The thing is she just wasn't desperate for a man, although she'd been thinking lately how lonely it could be in such a remote place.

Chapter Ten

Mack had been struggling to make a viable income from his hundred acres in Glenorchy—it just wasn't sufficient land to make it work for him without a secondary income. If only he could have joined forces with his grandfather and it saddened him to think of past regrets. Perhaps he could try him once more—really convince him that he is now a passionate and skilled farmer in all the rudiments of sheep and cattle farming as well as proficient in breaking horses, thanks to Joel Grey.

It was the end of a long day as he finished hammering in the barn he had been transforming into a new home. It was taking shape thanks to the recent help of a few church members who assisted him with lining the walls. He had some regret over buying a new barn for his animals and keeping the old one for a home that was poorly insulated. But with extra help from his church friends, he'll complete his new dwelling in time for the worst of the winter so his stock will have shelter in the storms.

He drove his quad bike down by the river to bring some sheep into the barn ready for collection the next day. They were off to the meat works. His border collie, Bluey, from the litter of Joel Grey's dog, Casey was the best sheepdog Mack had ever seen and had become his close friend and companion—just like Zoro.

Mack had a special way with animals, unlike other farmers apart from Joel Grey. It was a great attribute to have in a high country farmer. Bluey took no time at all jumping on the back of the quad bike and rounding up the paddock of sheep which Mack had chased through the gate down towards the barn where for pick-up the next morning.

Once he'd enclosed them, he checked the water levels and pellets in the troughs.

When Mack had finished feeding and watering the flock, he drove alongside the paddock where Zoro grazed. The animal saw him coming and trotted towards the gate. Looking down at the horse's shoulder, Mack could see that his wound had completely healed and offered him a carrot.

He loved working Zoro on the hills. He was a sure-footed animal and intelligent. Mack always rode the high country extra carefully on the quad bike. He didn't trust the machine on the steep, rugged slopes and usually only used it in the lower foothills.

He leaned over the fence looking straight at Zoro. 'What do you think of working on a large high country station, my boy? Can we handle it? The old man will probably say no again—but what if he says yes?' With that, Zoro pushed him hard in the chest with his head playfully and stood staring at him. It was as if he was saying yes—at least, that's what Mack was thinking. He decided to make one last attempt at trying to get hold of Walter and that evening he wrote him a letter.

The next morning Mack was sad to see his mature flock of sheep being sent off to the meat works. This was something new for him and he had regrets at cutting their lives short. It was so different from being a sheep shearer. But he convinced himself that farmers have a great role to play in feeding and clothing families and communities. He saw it as a necessity. No room for human emotion. One thing was for sure—he was going to be a humanitarian farmer and take care of his animals. Now there were fewer sheep to muster, the farm seemed kind of quiet although Mack still had a few hundred cattle. He hadn't yet built up his stock levels to a viable level on his hundred acres.

Chapter Eleven

Walter Reed had almost finished for the day. He'd been in the office with Aron Bendon his Station Manager discussing how to replace him. Aron had just resigned after thirteen years of managing Reed Station in the Dart Valley. His pregnant wife was near her time and so he'd decided to move them nearer to her family and a smaller station where he wouldn't be working such long hours. He planned to be able to enjoy some family time.

Walter had been about to tell him that he was also pulling back on account of his health and that Aron was going to have a lot more responsibility.

'This is no game for an old fella like me, Aron. This is the life for a young man. I don't know what I'm going to do as there aren't many young folk around here, let alone strong, young Station Managers.'

'Gee, I'm really sorry, Walter, but I've got to put my family first. I always told them I would. My wife, Sally is going to have twins and will need some help.'

'I know—I get you. But what am I going to do? I've such a substantial station here, I need a good manager.'

'You'll have to advertise. People all over New Zealand will see the advertisements. Doesn't have to be someone from around here.'

'And I've got to do all that interviewing and stuff. I'm past all that.'

'Well, I'm not going for a month. I'm sure I can help you with all that. We can interview them together.'

'I'll get going now. Don't bother getting up.'

'Actually, it's time for my afternoon nap in my hammock, so I'll follow you out onto the veranda.'

As the sun sank deep behind the mountain range, Walter waved to Aron who was on his way home to the station hand's cottage a mile down the road. He slid into his hammock on the covered veranda and pulled a piece of notepaper out of his pocket after putting on his dusty spectacles. He squinted then removed them, wiping the dust off with the sleeve of his Swaandri and placed them back on again. Even then, he struggled to see the details on the paper—

Mack Reed
RD Dart River Valley
Phone 03 123....

Walter grimaced then pulled his glasses off briskly. He let out a loud sigh. 'Darn! Stupid paper.'

The notepaper had got wet in his pocket when he'd been hosing out some stockyards and half the phone number was illegible. He struggled out of the hammock and walked into his kitchen where the light bulb was flickering. 'Huh! That confounded thing needs replacing already!' He pulled open a drawer and took out a writing pad and pen and then sat back at the dining table. Before the kitchen light went out, he quickly scratched a quick note, wrote urgent on the envelope and placed the letter inside.

Dear Mack

I think it's time we started to talk about business. When can you get here? If you are still interested, get in touch as soon as you can.

Walter Reed

Mack couldn't believe his eyes when he tore open the envelope he'd received later in the week. His heart raced. He could feel his pulse pounding in his temples and wanted to yell out and tell the world about the possible breakthrough.

'Thank you, God. I knew you wouldn't let me down. I've been patiently waiting for you to act and now you're finally coming through for me.' Mack had the first-hand experience of God often coming through in the eleventh hour.

What his grandfather intended for him was an enigma. Will they get on together? He was busting to ring and tell Jessie. Instead, he waited until he had spoken with Walter.

Sleep was elusive that night. He had stoked up the wood burner before going to bed, but the bone-chilling cold still penetrated him. The large corrugated iron barn was hot in summer and cold in winter. Although the building was insulated, the internal walls were not finished. It wouldn't be long though, as his church had promised him a working bee would be there at the end of the month.

After tossing and turning for an hour, he got up and put the kettle on to make a hot drink. He sat in his armchair with his mug, fantasising how life could be on a large station. Is this his dream come true? An hour later his head started to droop, and he almost spilt the remains of the Milo drink when he jolted awake. Half asleep, he put the mug in the kitchen and got back into bed.

He prayed, Please, God, grant me the serenity to accept the things I cannot change

Courage to change the things I can, and the wisdom to know the difference.

With that, he fell into a deep, peaceful sleep.

***

Jessie walked into the General Store almost knocking over the whole magazine stand with her bulky, leather shopping bag. She was in a hurry to gather her fortnight's supply of groceries before she started her working day.

She bent over to pick up the magazines she'd knocked to the floor. As she replaced them on the shelf, one, in particular, caught her attention—the new edition of the Australasian Veterinary Journal with a photo of a mobile veterinary clinic.

'Mmm, just what I need,' she muttered as she hauled the overloaded bag of supplies onto the counter.

'Goodness! You need a packhorse for that lot. Mind you, I won't complain. You've become a cherished regular customer of mine. I'll help you out to your vehicle with it if you like.'

'Aw, thanks, Mr Barnaby. I don't want to wear myself out before my rounds. I have a few farms to visit out this way and thought I'd do it all at once.'

'Just call me Barney—everyone else does. Though my first name is John, I've become rather partial to Barney.'

Jessie sensed the warmth in his voice. He was like most of the locals—friendly and helpful whenever possible, except for a miserable minority.

'Are you taking the magazine, Miss?' He pointed to the one she still held in her hand after she'd paid for the goods.

'Oh, stupid of me. I forgot about that. Yes, I'll take it.'

'Tell you what. You can have this one on me this time. Perhaps my old cat may need you someday and you might give me a discount.'

Jessie beamed, revealing a mouth full of well-cared-for teeth while Barney helped her out to the vehicle with her groceries.

'Thanks, Barney. I'd better get on my way. See you in a fortnight.'

He waved and went back inside the store.

Jessie fossicked around on the floor below the passenger seat. She'd brought a chilly bin for her meat and dairy products, although the outside temperature was getting cold enough to keep it cool.

Looking at her diary, there were three farms to visit—the first one being McKlintoch's Red Deer farm.

***

Doug McKlintoch called out roughly to his farm dog to get out of the way as Jessie approached his old Queenslander homestead. Doug stomped over towards Jessie's vehicle. She hesitated, not knowing where best to park. She glanced over towards the red-faced Scotsman who stood stiffly with his burly arms folded, eyeballing her. 'Over here! Park next to the shed, woman,' he shouted.

With that onslaught, a warm flush of blood rushed up her neck to her face. She was livid at being yelled out by the rude farmer when he'd never set eyes on her before. She wanted to turn around and take off back down the rough, stone driveway, as he didn't deserve a house call. But she had a responsibility towards the animals which were all under her care, just as most of the farm animals in the area had been previously under Max's care. This was her lot, and she had to either get used to it or go back to being a small animal vet in the city. She banished the thought immediately.

'Sorry, Mr McKlintoch. I didn't see you waving at me as I drove in and I certainly wasn't aware you had planted fresh grass seed over there.'

His frown relaxed as he beckoned her to follow him around the back of the house to a small enclosure with a high wire mesh for treating the stag.

'It's his front leg on the left side there.'

'Can I get inside? I mean—is he tame enough to approach?'

'Of course, you've no worries there. This one likes a good scratch under the antlers, but you need to keep watching how he moves his head and keep your face away from them.'

'Well, I have to sedate him, anyway. If you could get him ready for me please.'

Jessie dived into her bag to take out the sedative injection she had already prepared.

Within minutes the over-towering animal had gone down and Jessie quickly went to work cleaning and stitching the leg.

'These stitches will just dissolve in a few weeks. I'll be back and check the wound then, and in the meantime, you'll need to keep an eye out for any infection.'

In no time at all, Jessie had packed her bag up and after making another appointment to return, she started walking back to her vehicle, not wanting to stay a minute longer.

'By the way—how long are you filling in for Max? When are they getting a permanent bloke out here?'

Jessie couldn't get away from the insensitive farmer quick enough. He was the worst she'd met so far, of all the mean spirited, misogynistic farmers. She had already come across several but that wasn't really a lot considering the size of the Glenorchy community. Most of the farmers she'd met had been kind and supportive of her new role. But the ones who weren't, made her life a misery.

'I'm sorry to disappoint you, but I am it! And you'll have to get used to me, I'm afraid!' she huffed.

Red-faced, she stomped towards the Land Rover. She roughly threw her bag onto the passenger seat and climbed in fighting the surging anger that choked her. When she started the engine, about to drive off in a fury, Doug hastened towards the driver's door.

'Wait—I forgot to say thanks for helping out ... I should have asked you in for a cup of tea. My wife is away up north visiting the grandchildren ... otherwise, she would have invited you in.'

The choking feeling around her neck seemed to subside after he showed her a more human side. He didn't ask her in, to her relief. She wasn't sure about him—a vulnerable young woman with a lonely farmer in such a remote area.

'That's okay, I have to move on. I've no time for cups of tea.'

While driving to the next farm, she prayed for the grace to accept the ignorance and male chauvinism of these high country farmers. They were victims of generational brainwashing. She was determined to win them over and become as well accepted in her new community as Max had been.

***

The next visit went a lot smoother than the previous one. The farmer had a herd of Angora goats which he had reared himself. One of the nannies had an udder infection which Jessie had been treating with antibiotics. She needed to check it regularly.

As she drove up to the farm, she started to imagine that if she had a mobile clinic down on the flat in Glenorchy, some of these farmers could transport their smaller animals to the clinic. That would save her from having to make many long trips in one day to the remote high country farms. She would definitely do some investigating on that subject.

The goat farmer, Bob, although not over-friendly did not treat her badly. He just never smiled and appeared to have no sense of humour. But this time, as she said goodbye, he handed her a bottle of goat's milk and a lump of feta cheese wrapped in muslin as she started her engine. His wife, Alma ran a small cottage industry of products made from goat's milk as well as using their wool which she sold to craft shops in Queenstown.

It was after nine in the evening by the time Jessie had finished her rounds. She'd spent far too long with Bob and Alma and hadn't even eaten. She headed back down the Glenorchy-Paradise Road towards home—BANG! Her vehicle swerved off the road, skidding on the loose stones and coming to a halt in a small ditch. Although she wore a seatbelt, the impact had winded her. She sat in her seat clutching at her chest, trying to recover from the shock. She stretched her neck sideways. 'Ow, not a whiplash as well,' she cried out.

She stumbled, almost falling when she opened the driver's door to take a look at the vehicle. 'Oh no, why now?' She glared at the

70

rear tyre that had gone completely flat. As she looked closer, she could see a large nail poking out of the rubber.

'Dear Lord this is unbelievable. Why do these things have to happen at night?' She spoke almost angrily as if she was admonishing her maker for allowing it to happen. But that wasn't in her nature to hold resentment towards God.

She shone the torch on the Carphone on the dashboard, picked up the handpiece and dialled the Vet Call Centre.

'I'm stuck on the Glenorchy-Paradise Road, just past the Priory Road turnoff heading south. There's a nail in my tyre and it's pitch black out here. Can you send someone to help me?'

The Call Centre Operator asked her to hold on while she looked down the list to see which farmer lived close to Jessie's location.

'It looks like Sam Grimsley is closest to you. I'll call him and send him over to you.'

Oh, no, thought Jessie. He was one of the nasty members of the High Country Farmers Association who was Doug McKlintoch's buddy and who'd also given her a hard time.

'Is he the only one nearest to me? Is there anyone else as I don't think he'd be too keen if you called him out at this hour?'

Time was flying by and Jessie was aware that most farmers go to bed early. *It must be at least nine-thirty now and hardly anybody would be still up.*

'No, sorry, Jessie. There is Jerry Lynes and his wife is ill. I can't phone him.'

Perhaps she should have contacted Mack. He would always help her but this time, she didn't want him to think she was just a helpless female. Or did she have too much pride?

'Oh—okay, then. It will just have to be Sam,' mumbled Jessie though the speaker.

'I'll stay on the radio until he arrives if you would rather,' said the operator. 'I'll let you know if he's unable to help you. If I can't get hold of him, I'll find someone else, or I'll phone the local police constable if there's nobody available.'

'That's kind of you, but I think I'll be okay … except for the batteries on this Carphone that are going flat. I'll just keep the door locked. The locals say that nothing happens out here.'

When she hung up the receiver, she sat in her vehicle looking out across at the Richardson mountain range in the distance. Although it was dark, the snow-capped peaks glistened, boasting pastels of pink and purple in the light of the full moon. She carried a camera in her vehicle to snap the spectacular scenes in and around Glenorchy whenever she could and wanted to jump out of the car to snap this one but she pulled back. There was an eeriness that existed in the dead stillness of the night as she noticed formidable shadows dancing in the reflection of the mountains. Suddenly she caught a glimpse of a small light flashing in the distance coming rapidly towards her. Her heart pounded and missed a few beats. She froze in her seat. *There could be all kinds of weird people wandering around out here.*

She fought back her wild imagination and tried to cast unsettling thoughts out of her mind by whispering a short prayer. After that, a thought came to her. *Mack, I'll call him. Let's face it— this is an emergency—he shouldn't mind.*

She picked up her Carphone again and tried to get hold of him but there was no reception. The batteries had run out.

'Oh no! Not now please, God.'

She'd forgotten to recharge the batteries the evening before. Up until now, she'd always recharged them with the charger in her office before going to bed each night just as Max had instructed her

She tried not to panic and before she broke out in a cold sweat, the advancing small light had suddenly become large as bright headlights suddenly dazzled her. Within an hour, to her relief, a noisy truck pulled alongside her, the vehicle's lights blinding her. The driver wound down his window and Jessie did the same.

'Jessie, the vet, isn't it? Just heard from the Call Centre to say you're in trouble.'

'Ah … not exactly in trouble. I have a puncture and can't see to repair it.'

Sam muttered something under his breath and shifted his truck so that the headlights shone on her vehicle's wheels.

Jessie stepped out and pulled her spare wheel from the back. Sam grabbed it and rolled it towards the rear wheels.

'I don't think we've met,' she murmured, hoping to break the ice.

'That'll be right. I bring my smaller animals to the clinic in Closeburn and Robbie Byrnes comes out here to my farm whenever I need him. I haven't had any need for your services.'

Jessie swallowed the lump in her throat and coughed. Her blood pressure rose at his obvious discrimination of her—frustrated by her sense of defeat at that moment. She prayed for courage and determination to rise above it as she was definitely going to have to do that if she wanted to continue practising as a vet in the high country. If only she had a sign, a sure indication from God that this was her calling. Her veterinary friends and colleagues had made it clear to her that in order for her to function well as a remote high country vet it would have to be a divine calling. Otherwise, it would just be too hard.

It didn't take him long to change the tyre. 'I'd be getting myself an extra spare if you plan to continue running around out here at night. You wouldn't want to be stranded. Lucky I came along, eh?'

'Yes, you're right. I'll make sure I do that. I'm so sorry to get you out here at this time of night. Thanks a lot.'

He fitted the damaged tyre back into its space on the back of the vehicle. 'Well, there you are, all done. I suggest you get this one repaired as soon as possible. In fact, even the one I swapped it with is not too great, so make sure you get onto it.'

He rubbed his hands together as if to clean them, wiping them on his overalls.

Sam was being respectful, contrary to his convictions about female vets. Jessie started warming to the old fella in a way she'd not thought possible after their first meeting.

'Thanks again. I owe you. Let me offer you some free vaccinations or consultation sometime.'

'Mmm ... I'll give it a thought. You'd better get off now. I'll follow you until you get nearer Glenorchy, just to make sure that tyre's going to be alright.'

Jessie accepted his offer and guessed he had a touch of humanity. Perhaps he too could change. She would have to pray for him—another grumpy farmer to add to her prayer list.

She wiggled her neck. Thankfully the pain had settled. She hadn't sustained a whiplash but was shaken. Stranded on an isolated road in the dark, alone for almost an hour. *It won't happen again. God forbid!*

Chapter Twelve

Mack knocked on the old solid oak door. He rubbed his hand over the unusual knot in the wood that gave the gnarled door a rustic appearance. No one came. He knocked harder this time. He was sure he had the right day. He glanced at his watch—he was dead on time. He heard the pounding of hooves nearby and turned around. A horseman who appeared to be one of the station hands trotted towards him.

'Gidday, mate—Mack, isn't it? Your grandfather's expecting you. He's on his way. Ben's the name. We had trouble with one of the water bores that got blocked with ice. He said to show you into his office. You can wait there.'

The horseman flung himself out of the saddle and tied his chestnut mare to the railing in front of the dated, wooden colonial homestead that needed a coat of white paint. Mack followed him up the steps and onto the porch where Ben shook off his high leather riding boots and Mack followed suit.

'Take a seat in here. He's just along the track in his truck. I'll leave you to it if you don't mind. There are some young steers up the back I need to shift and a couple of our station hands are at the Agricultural Show today. Can I give you a beer?'

'Oh, no, thanks mate. I'm okay. Don't drink the stuff—it doesn't agree with me. Catch you another time.'

By the time Ben had unhitched his horse and cantered off, Walter had stepped out of his truck and headed for the office. Mack rubbed his abdomen as if to relieve the knot the tension had caused—the stress of the build-up to this special day he had hoped and dreamed of for years. *Take a deep breath ... keep on breathing*, he kept telling himself.

The sight of the tall, frail-looking farmer with blond turned grey hair and weathered skin that looked like an old leather handbag made his eyes smart. He fought back the uncontrollable moisture oozing from his eyes.

'Mack! Thanks for coming.' Walter lunged forward to shake Mack's hand with a strong, firm handshake that impressed him.

'Stay seated. Can I get you a beer or coffee, maybe?'

'Thanks, but I don't drink ale. I'm okay thanks. I had a coffee before I left home.'

'Well ... let's get down to the brass tacks. I guess you are wondering why I've asked you here ... well, it's not exactly for a social visit. It's hard for me to say but I need some help.'

Mack fixed his gaze on the aged man's face—a profile that told a thousand tales of times past. He saw that his estranged kin was lost for words and attempted to rescue him.

'Sorry, do you mean with the station or you personally?'

Mack's thick eyebrows curled and a furrow formed in his brow. He spoke with a croak in his voice.

'This place, of course.' He pointed towards the green rolling hills. 'All two thousand acres of it. You see ... my health hasn't been good for the last few years and I've been struggling. I have a great Station Manager—Aron is his name, but he has resigned. His wife is about to produce twins and he needs to help his family. He's moving to the McKenzie country to work as a leading farmhand on a small sheep station.'

Mack's heart gave an extra beat. 'Oh, really? What are you going to do? It's a big job for you on your own.'

'I've got four station hands. but none of them is manager material. I've heard through the grapevine a great deal about your farming skills and capabilities. I'm hoping you might be the right man for the job. Let me see those bits of paper you've brought me.'

Mack dived into his leather satchel and pulled out a Manilla folder full of documents.

'As this is one of the smaller stations in the area, you would actually be a head shepherd as well as Station Manager. I can still manage the books but I'll eventually need to employ a bookkeeper.'

It's strange he doesn't mention anything about Dad or why he hasn't been in touch all these years. Mack's throat had dried up. He struggled to swallow while forcing himself to relax and breathe as he thrust the file into Walter's hands. Five minutes later Walter handed it back to him while he sat painfully still for every minute.

'Right, follow me. I'm going to take you for a drive. I can't show you the whole station, but you will be able to get a good idea of the size and capacity of the station. I'll introduce you to any of the workers if I see them. You've already met my leading station hand, Ben. You can always rely on him.' Walter's gruff, commanding manner irritated Mack. Would he be able to tolerate this cantankerous old farmer? He would have to win him over somehow. Still, he's waited so long for such a break-through he will just have to practise some long-suffering with God's help.

After a busy morning seeing most of the station, either by truck, horseback or by farm bike, Mack returned to the homestead overwhelmed. Walter shook off his gumboots at the front door while Mack pulled off his leather boots and followed Walter into the lounge. Walter offered him a seat while Mack looked around at what appeared to be a time-warp of memorabilia on the walls and scattered about the room. These were photographs and artefacts of Mack's great grandfather, the gold miner before he purchased Reed Station. The black and white photos impressed Mack.

'Ah yes—you wouldn't have seen any of these I suppose. I don't think your father has any.'

'No, he hasn't. I've never seen them before.'

'Take a look over here.' Walter walked over to the fireplace and on the wall was a large photo of what appeared to be Reed Station when it was first purchased and a substantial white colonial mansion that no longer existed.

'Wow—that must take you back. I guess you'd be able to write a book about that heritage. It's very interesting.'

'Yeah well ... your father never took any interest. But there's a book over here that one of the Historical Trusts has published. It has a lot in there about the Reed family history. You must take a look sometime, but first of all, we need to get back to brass tacks. I want to know what you think and more so how you feel about managing a station this size. I'll be around still to help you out and advise you as long as the old ticker keeps going.' He winked at Mack who sat on the edge of his seat, eyes wide.

'To be perfectly honest with you, I'm completely blown away by the awesomeness of this place. It's amazing and it would be a huge privilege for me to manage this for you. I'm a bit dumbfounded by your offer.'

'Oh, forget all that palaver. Are you willing to take it on or not?'

His curtness upset Mack. He tried to stretch his neck muscles to ease the tension caused by his grandfather's abrasiveness. *Why is he so abrupt? What has made him so hard and rigid? A smile would crack his face.*

'Absolutely, without a doubt. When would you want me to start?'

'It would have to be pretty soon, as Aron is staying for a month to orientate you before he leaves.'

'That's no problem, I'll start next week. I'll have to work with Aron part-time while I'm winding up my own property. I need to sell the cattle and sheep I have left and once I've settled in here, I'll sell the farm. Then there's my stallion, Zoro. He's my workhorse.'

'What about bringing the stock over here? Load them up on a truck and the station can buy them from you. Just write down how many animals you have and their details. I'll let the accountant know. I don't handle that side of things.'

Mack sat wringing his hands—the tension in his neck beginning to cause pain until Walter walked over to him and put out his hand. Mack took it eagerly as Walter shook it hard. After this act of humanity, Mack was able to relax.

'Wow, that's a really generous offer—thanks very much. The cattle are healthy and almost fat enough for the meat works. The sheep are merino like yours and will make you proud.'

'It's time for a good feed. My house-keeper, Bessie, usually cooks a hot meal at midday but it will be a little late today. The station hands also partake in a meal in the other dining room. I think lamb hotpot is on the menu today. Come on, I'll have to introduce you to her.'

'Mmm, it sure smells good. Thanks for everything ... um, I don't know what to call you?'

'I'm your grandfather, aren't I? You call me, Grandad, okay? But whatever you do, don't start calling me gramps.' Walter almost broke a weak smile.

The two men had broken the ice. They wandered down the long hallway to the old farmhouse kitchen where Bessie was waiting for them. Walter introduced Bessie to Reed Station's new manager then led him to the dining room. He seated Mack next to him at a long solid oak table which had been attractively laid with all the attributes of farmhouse cuisine including old world bone china. Once again Mack's eyes starting to smart with salty moisture which he forced back.

This was a long-awaited answer to prayer and the joy in his heart that bubbled over was indescribable. This was the first day of a whole new chapter in his life. But where did his friend, Jessie fit in? Had she now disappeared into insignificance? Only time would tell.

Chapter Thirteen

A Month Later

The snow had thawed on the foothills surrounding her home but remained on the mountain tops. It was an awesome sight as Jessie went hiking alone high up onto the ridge near her home. It was a fresh morning early in spring as she stumbled up the well-trodden rough track to the top. From there she was able to look over the surrounding farms and in the distance, she could see as far as Paradise and Mount Earnslaw. Spring and autumn were her favourite seasons. In spring she loved to watch the birds come to life after a long hard winter as they fluttered about searching for seeds.

She sat on a rock with her eyes fixed on the tender green leaves on the Poplar trees. A wave of nostalgia came over her—memories of pencil-shaped Poplars that lined the paddocks on her parents' farm.

For the first time since she had arrived in Glenorchy, she was fighting pangs of homesickness. Minutes later, as she fixed her gaze onto the majestic snow-capped mountains and watched a large Kea bird flying overhead, she remembered what it was that kept her there. The mountains had called her once and right now they continued to pull at her heartstrings again. The nostalgia for Bethlehem soon left her, as she set off down the track towards home.

As she tugged at her boots at the front door, she was sure she heard the phone ring, then stop. It was her usual day off and the

Call Centre would divert her business calls. It didn't ring again. She knew Hope and Cole had gone to a horse breeder's convention in Queenstown and wouldn't be back till late that night. Oh well, she thought. If it's really important, they'll phone again.

She still needed the wood fire and managed to get it going with the small pile of wood she had left. The load of firewood Mack had delivered to her was running out and she would still need another load to last her through spring. It got pretty cold in these parts and heating the whole house with a small electric heater was too costly. Perhaps she should give him a call and pay him a visit as it had been some time since she'd last heard from him. He'd told her he was busy with his renovations and taking stock to the auctions. But Jessie thought he had gone unusually quiet.

I know—I'll pay him a surprise visit and take over some of my Apple Crumble he likes so much. She rallied around looking for a dish for the dessert she had frozen and packed it into a basket with several fresh muffins. She had always baked on her day off and she'd made this batch early that morning.

The thought of visiting her friend, Mack, put an extra spring in her step as she busied herself trying to coordinate her denim jeans with the right woollen jumper. She tried on a tomato red, soft Cashmere top that contrasted perfectly with the blue denim. Next, she pulled on the new tan suede boots with high heels—the pair she'd brought home from the General Store earlier in the week. It was one of her few opportunities to wear them, as her social life was lacking in Glenorchy.

She climbed into the Land Rover that she now owned, thanks to Max. He had offered it to her for a most reasonable price on his return from holiday, as he and his wife had agreed to upgrade their vehicle. The Land Rover was just right for Jessie. It even had plenty of room in the back for her to be able to sleep when staying overnight in Queenstown, once she'd got rid of the doggy smell. It was something she'd always imagined driving.

As she carefully veered around the icy corner towards Mack's driveway entrance, the vehicle almost skidded as she slammed her foot on the brakes and screeched to a standstill next to a large sign on the gate. With her hands frozen on the steering wheel, her eyes narrowed as she leaned her head towards the windscreen.

There in front of her stood a sign that read, "Farm for Sale". *Why hadn't he said anything to me about this?*

The poached eggs and bacon she'd eaten earlier started swimming their way up her gullet. She willed the sick feeling away and drove hastily through the large puddles along the driveway towards Mack's homestead. His old tractor was parked next to the animal barn. She climbed out of her vehicle and looked around. There was an eerie silence as she glanced the extensive rows of paddocks. There was not an animal in sight. Usually, she would hear the barking of a working dog, and Zoro, his horse was usually in the front paddock next to the home. Mack had always kept him close by since the stallion's abduction, but she couldn't see him anywhere.

He wouldn't just suddenly leave without telling me. What's got into him? Mind you, I've been so run off my feet lately and haven't had time for anyone. Perhaps it was he who was ringing me. She knocked on his front door then went around to the back. She even wandered over to the large animal barn and still nothing. All the animals had gone. Stumbling on hard green cowpats, she raced back to Mack's homestead that appeared to be completely renovated—the first time Jessie had seen it in months. When she peered through the windows, her heart sank and that same sick feeling came over her. All of Mack's household contents had gone. The place looked bare except for scanty items of furniture. *He's moved away and without a word. What on earth happened? I must get home and phone Hope and Cole. They'll know.*

Why was she feeling so upset? She asked herself. They weren't in a relationship, just good friends, or so she thought—or was she in denial about her real feelings? Her eyes smarted as she drove bleary-eyed back to her cottage whispering a prayer to ask God to shed some light on Mack's disappearance.

***

82

Cole answered the phone. 'Hi, Jessie. Haven't heard from you in a while. Hope has phoned you a few times.'

'Oh, really? I had no idea. That makes me think I really have to buy one of those flash Phone Mate answer machines.'

'Bertie's been missing you,' he laughed. 'He's put on so much weight. Hope took him to the Plunket Nurse in Glenorchy this week.'

Jessie loved to hear about little Bertie but she was busting to say what she had phoned about.

'Um ... I've been trying to get hold of Mack as Zoro's vaccinations are due soon. I've just been to the farm, and it appears to be for sale. There's a large sign at the gate and there's no sign of any animals. His home is bare too.' Her voice quavered even though she tried hard to stop it.

'Oh, no. Mack said he would phone you and let you know. I'd assumed he'd done that.'

'He should have contacted me through the Vet Call Centre. They could have located me on my radio phone.'

'I expect he didn't think it appropriate if it was a personal call.'

'Where has he gone?'

'To work for his grandfather who offered him the job of Station Manager.'

'Wow, really? On that two thousand acre farm! That's so amazing. Did he sell all his stock?'

'No, his grandfather bought the stock and Mack's using Zoro as his workhorse. Why don't you go out there and see him? You said you need to vaccinate Zoro. Hold on ... I'll just get the address and phone number. You can decide if you want to phone first or take pot luck and drive out there.'

Jessie's hand shook as she scribbled the address.

'I ... suppose so. Thanks, Cole. Is Hope able to come to the phone for a quick word?'

'Oh, sorry. She's taken Bertie into Glenorchy for his vaccinations. Pity you can't give them.'

'Ha, not likely. Anyone can deliver a baby but I have to be certified to give people vaccinations.'

'I'll tell Hope you called. Maybe she can call you later this evening for a girl's chinwag,' he chuckled.

It had been an eventful day but not a relaxing one as Jessie had anticipated. Later that evening she rearranged her diary to fit in the visit to Reed Station in Dart Valley the next day. There were some other horses in the area to vaccinate so she thought she may as well do Zoro too. Fortunately for her, she had been able to build up quite a large clientele in the district not too far from her home. Before she settled into bed that evening, the phone rang. She almost jumped out of her skin then remembered Cole had said he would get Hope to call her. It was her, and the two chatted until late catching up on all their girly news.

'Well, I really think you need to go to Reed Station tomorrow,' said Hope. 'Mack has done a quite a bit of sheep shearing here for my father in the last month and said he had tried to call you a few times to let you know he was moving. Just go and surprise him. Let me know how you get on. And by the way—can you help with a bit of babysitting this weekend? We've got a wedding to attend and you're so good with Bertie. Or would you rather we ask one of the older girls from church?'

'Sure, I'll do it. I'll call you later in the week to confirm.'

'And to let me know all the juicy gossip about Mack.' They both laughed. The phone call lifted her spirit. Her face glowed and excited expectation infiltrated her soul.

Chapter Fourteen

Spring started to announce its arrival. The sun forced its way between her bedroom curtains, falling on her shoulders as she soaked up its warmth while she was dressing. There was an eagerness in her heart today. She was keen to hear all about Mack's wonderful new role as Station Manager, but more so, how he was getting on with his grandfather. It would be a dream come true for him. It annoyed her that he hadn't been able to get hold of her by phone. He wasn't the kind of man who would leave her guessing. She wondered if she should put the Apple Crumble she had baked for him into the chilly bin with the lunch she'd packed for herself. But what if he wasn't there? She'd only have to bring the dish home again. She decided against it. Anyway—perhaps he had more interesting things to think about than her Apple Crumble. She quickly banished the idea.

By lunchtime, she'd finished the visits to both the smaller farms on Glenorchy-Paradise Road. She stopped her vehicle in a pull-in by the Beech forest, her preferred spot where she found peace and tranquillity. It reminded her of the horse-treks she used to take with her friend, Hope before she had married Cole. Now their lives had changed so much—Hope with a baby and herself a busy vet.

She unwound the car window and focused her gaze on the forest where they used to see the wild horses come down to the lake to drink and remembered the time they had seen a mare with her foal. She would love to have her own land and keep a few horses, as she grew up with them. How she missed those times, but Hope had said she can ride their horses any time she liked.

She was distracted by what she thought was a black horse. Or was it just that she'd been daydreaming about horses? No, her eyes did not deceive her. Near the lake by the entrance to the extensive red beech forest, stood a tall black horse drinking at the water's edge. Its sleek coat glistened in the sun and it appeared oblivious to a group of picnickers sitting at a table nearby. She wanted to go over and take a photo but knew that by the time she drove over to the horse, it would be gone. This wonderful memory will just have to stay in the back of her mind for safe-keeping.

Glancing at her watch, it was time to visit Reed Station. The sandwiches she had bolted down seemed to stick in her throat as the anxiety built at the thought of driving out there uninvited, but it was now or never.

***

As Jessie was about to turn into the long driveway that led to Reed Station, she turned on the windscreen wiper to clear the thick layer of dust that had settled on the window when a vehicle had driven passed her through a puddle earlier. The water made it worse. Now it was just a muddy mess, and it blurred her vision. This is the life of a rural vet, she reminded herself. She stopped the vehicle and pulled out an old rag to give it a good wipe then climbed back into the vehicle.

She drove on up to the nostalgic colonial homestead minus the picket fence. Climbing roses would have suited that style of home, she imagined. There was an old hay baler in one corner and Mack's Ute parked nearby.

She banged on the oak door. The house-keeper opened it and said, 'Well, well. It's the first time I've seen a woman on this station, apart from myself ... not for many years. Bessie's my name. What can I do for you?'

'Hello, Bessie. My name's Jessie. I'm the new vet and I'm looking for Mack. His horse's vaccinations are due.'

'Oh my goodness. You're the one they've been chatting about. Mack has tried to get hold of you. He'll be pleased to see you, as he's worried about you. His grandfather, Walter has had some concerns about one or two animals this week and hasn't got around to calling the Vet Cooperative yet. Come on in,' she said as she directed her into the lounge.

'Mack is on his horse below that ridge up there by the pine trees. A steer fell into a creek and he's had to free it. He hasn't taken his radiophone with him as he said he wouldn't be away long. Walter should be around somewhere mending fences. He's not far away either as he usually comes in for lunch and hasn't eaten yet. He'll be on his quad bike somewhere.'

Jessie smiled while she observed the robust friendly woman, someone she could warm to easily.

'If you don't mind, I'll have to keep going. I'll go and look for them. How far can I take my vehicle up there?' Jessie asked.

'Most of the way up that track, and when you get to the first long wooden gate, you can go through it, but you'll have to go by foot. Mack will be across that paddock over there just before the creek. It's a bit of a walk, mind you, but when you see Zoro, his horse, you'll be in the right place. Or maybe it'll be better to wait here until he comes in.'

'Oh, I'll be fine. I've strong walking boots and I need the exercise. I spend a lot of time in my vehicle.'

'Please come back with him for a cup of tea,' she said, retying her apron.

Jessie thanked her for the directions and got back into her vehicle. She drove slowly up the dirt track that led to the large wooden gate that Bessie described. The track was longer than she had imagined which was understandable as she was only used to farms the size of her father's four hundred acre farm. The paddocks on a station this size were huge in comparison.

'Ah, this must be the gate,' she muttered as she stopped suddenly. She scanned as far as her eye could see and there was no sign of Mack. She got out and wandered up and down the track searching again full circle. Nothing. She was afraid to drive on in case she got lost in the maze of numerous side roads and tracks between vast paddocks. Then something black caught her eye on the opposite side in the distance. She got back in the vehicle and drove as far as she could until she found a gate on that side and got out. It was a black horse, and it appeared to hang its head over something lying on the ground. She grabbed her medical bag, put her Stetson on her head, and started walking. As she drew closer after a five-minute walk, she recognised the horse. It was Zoro without a rider. 'Oh no, it's not Mack lying there, is it?' She spouted, loudly. The horse seemed to be nudging what appeared to her to be a man lying on the ground. The stallion was gently licking and butting him with his head. But the figure definitely wasn't Mack. As she hurried towards the scene, she saw an elderly man lying on the ground. Zoro towered over him licking his face and hands repeatedly trying to keep his body warm. The horse then started rubbing his head up and down Walter's body. There was snow on the surrounding hilltops and the ground was still ice-cold for late spring.

Jessie rushed to the man's side then patted the horse's nose. 'Thank you, Zoro. You've been trying to help him.'

As she examined the lifeless man he moaned. From her examination, she ascertained that he'd likely suffered a stroke.

She dived into her medical bag after turning him on his side to help his breathing and then tried to use her radiophone. There was just a lot of static. She had to get assistance. 'You stay here with him, Zoro. I'll go for help.'

Before she went off, she'd realised that the hay that covered the aged man's body was not from the farmer carrying it, as there was no bale anywhere near. She'd seen one by the open gate when she had raced over to him. It must have been Zoro who had gathered the hay from there and spread it over the victim's body to keep him warm.

She bent over and gathered up the loose straw that had fallen off when she had turned him onto his side and covered his torso and legs with it.

Jessie guessed that the old man was probably Walter as the tools on the ground next to him were reminiscent of fencing tools.

She raced back and alerted Bessie who was able to radio one of the station hands to find Mack. Bessie then contacted the doctor and the air ambulance.

Jessie hurried back in her vehicle to Walter with a rug that Bessie had given her and waited until Mack turned up. As she ran across the paddock with the rug, Zoro was still standing over Walter like a sentry on guard. He was licking every bit of skin that was exposed on Walter's body. The horse whinnied softly when Jessie returned and nudged her arm gently as she covered Walter with the rug. He groaned then opened his eyes and stared at her, trying to speak, but his speech sounded garbled.

'Hello, Walter. I'm Jessie the new vet. I'm also a friend of Mack's and I think you've had a stroke and we're getting help. The air ambulance from Glenorchy is on its way, but the doctor will get here first.'

She placed a cushion she'd carried from her vehicle under his head. He tried to talk again with disjointed speech. 'Just you rest and try not to talk. You are going to be all right.'

Five minutes later, Mack arrived on a quad bike with a station hand sitting behind. He ran to his grandfather's side.

'Goodness me, Jessie! What brings you here—just in time? You've saved my grandfather.' He leaned over Walter and grabbed his hand. 'What happened to him?'

'It's not me you need to thank ... it's Zoro, here.' She patted the horse on the neck and let him lick her hand.

'Your faithful horse guarded Walter closely and kept him warm by spreading hay on his body. He's amazing, an angel. Unusual for a stallion. I think your grandfather has had a stroke, but I can't say for sure.'

Just at that moment, another quad bike with two men on it turned up at the gate. Mack rushed over to let them in. It was one of Mack's station hands with the doctor who raced to Walter's side. Within a short time, he confirmed the patient had suffered another stroke.

The air ambulance, a shiny red helicopter landed in the paddock next to Zoro's field. Before long, Walter was on his way to Queenstown Hospital. Mack stayed behind to manage the station.

'I should have taken my radiophone with me, but I was initially only going to help a steer stuck in a fence then I ventured further up the track on Zoro to check some other stock,' said Mack, as he and Jessie walked back to her vehicle. 'When I dismounted to take a look at some of my steers, Zoro took off down the track towards his paddock. He'd never done that before. I realise now that he knew something was wrong with Grandad who had been repairing the fence in Zoro's paddock. That's his quad bike over there.' He pointed to the track next to the paddock.

'That makes him a pretty special kind of stallion.'

'That's for sure. He surely saved Grandad's life. I won't go off without my radiophone again, though, I can assure you.'

'It's not me you need to assure.'

Mack climbed into Jessie's Land Rover. She drove him back to his homestead.

'What brings you here, anyway? I've tried to call you several times to let you know Grandad asked me to manage Reed Station, and I have put my farm up for sale,' Mack asked.

'I know. Cole told me and so did Bessie. I'm sorry, but I've been so busy and often don't get home until late. Next time, just phone the Vet Call Centre at the Co-op. They'll locate me. By the way— Zoro's vaccinations are due. That's why I'm here, just in case you've forgotten.'

'Oh, that's right. I knew they were due sometime soon. It's a bit much for you today. Thanks so much for helping Grandad. You came just in time. I'd appreciate it if you come again soon to vaccinate Zoro. You can always leave phone messages with Bessie.'

'I'll come back next week. I need to go home now. Give me a call when you want me to come back and do the vaccinations.'

'Aren't you going to come in for tea or coffee? We can have a good catch up.'

'Sorry, I really need to get going.' She couldn't get rid of the reasoning going on in her mind that if he genuinely wanted to see her, he could have called the Vet Call Centre and left a message.

'I'll be in touch soon. Zoro obviously recognised you,' said Mack. 'He'll look forward to seeing you.' He glanced at her with a sheepish grin. She tried to read between the lines. He was probably feeling guilty, but perhaps he had meant it.

***

Jessie was shaken up by the events of the day. She'd looked forward to a grand catch up with Mack and it had really turned to custard. Part of her had wanted to accept the invitation to stay for afternoon tea but the ordeal with Walter was exhausting. Her feet were aching, and she was sure she had pulled her calf muscle when she ran across the paddock with the blanket, tripping on thick tufts of grass and uneven ground.

When she arrived home, she tugged off her boots and crashed on her bed. She lay there thinking about the day's events and said a prayer for Walter. She prayed for healing—*Please, God, restore Walter to good health again. Have mercy on poor Mack as he has only just begun to unite with his grandfather. Let him be able to have a relationship with him that he has always longed for. Amen.*

Chapter Fifteen

Three weeks later, the hospital discharged Walter in good shape after a mild stroke. He had regained his speech and apart from some residual weakness down one side of his body, he walked with a limp. Mack was sure it was a miracle and the old man showed determination to help him run the station again.

Bessie had her work cut out running around after Walter more than usual. She kept a good eye on him making sure he followed the doctor's orders.

Early one evening, Walter sat under the awning of the veranda drinking tea from his beloved worn out mug that Bessie had handed him. He was discussing the future plans for the station with Mack who was enjoying a bottle of Bessie's new batch of ginger beer.

'I want you to hold on to this station, and maybe one day, if you have a family of your own, they might just be interested. I don't know how much longer I'll be active, with my health the way it is. You need to get yourself a wife to help you keep the place going.'

Mack turned and gaped at him as he picked up his glass. He spluttered, almost choking as he swallowed. 'There aren't many women in these parts who are still available, Grandad.'

'What about the young lassie who came to see me in hospital—that young vet you've been talking about? I was away with the fairies a bit when she came to see me, but I remember she was the one who found me. A lovely girl she is. She'd fit in well up here, don't you think?'

Mack cleared his throat and scuffed his boots under his seat back and forth. 'I haven't really given that any thought— I've been so busy. I don't think she would be interested, and if I marry, it will be for love and not a business proposition, Grandad.'

Walter's neck reddened. He went quiet for a moment.

'Sorry, Mack, I didn't mean to embarrass you. I should mind my own business. I just worry about how you will cope with this place on your own if I croak.'

'It's okay. We have reliable station hands and there's Bessie of course who has been here for years. She has part-time cooks she can all on if we have a lot of workers to feed. The ranch hands can pay for a hot meal which Bessie organises but they often look after themselves.'

'I can also ask experienced farmers like Joel Grey and Cole Rigby for advice. They don't have such an extensive property as we have, but they are some of the most skilled and notable farmers around here, according to Max, the vet who recently retired.'

'If you say so. Sounds like you have plenty of confidence, that's for certain. I'm sure you'll do just fine.'

'Hope you don't mind, but would you be able to give me a quick rundown of the history of Reed Station? I can't remember the chain of events leading up to you living here.'

'That's a good idea. Could you top up my mug first, please? We might be in for a long session. His eyes smiled at Mack.

'No problem, Grandad.'

While Mack took the mug into the kitchen, Walter's countenance changed. He started pulling at his fingers and wringing his hands. When Mack trundled onto the veranda with a fresh mug of tea, Walter was sitting at the small café table tapping his fingers. Sadness clouded his facial features.

'Good strong tea. Bessie's brew is always stewed—just how I like it. Now, you want to know all about the Reed family history.'

Bessie came out to the veranda.

'I think you'd better come in for a short nap before dinner, Walter.'

'Not now, Bessie. I'll be in a bit later. I think Mack and I are in for a lengthy session.'

Bessie got the message and scurried away.

Walter rubbed the nape of his neck then began—'Our ancestors had become wealthy during the Otago gold rush in Arrowtown. Some years later they purchased Reed Station. I met your grandmother, Hazel, in the McKenzie country near Lake Tekapo, where she grew up on a sheep farm. We married in the Church of the Good Shepherd near the lake. I worked as a farmhand on her father's farm. Several years later, following a severe drought, her parents lost all their livestock, and eventually their farm after they had gone bankrupt.'

'Wow. That's a hard blow. Where did you both go after that?'

'We came here as I inherited Reed Station at that time. Your grandmother and I had considered having a large family but conceived only one son, Len, your father.'

Walter looked around for his jacket which he found on the railing and put it on.

'It's getting a bit fresh now the sun's going down.' Mack rubbed his arms and shuddered. 'I'll just duck inside and put a jumper on.'

When he returned, Walter continued.

'The Reeds had been able to keep this station in the family for generations until your father had rejected my offer to help me manage it, heading off to university in Wellington instead.'

'I'll bet that was a lump of disappointment for you to swallow, your only son abandoning you in a way.'

'We'd had major arguments about his future plans upon graduating from university, but he was headstrong. When he moved to Wellington to set up a lucrative export business, he fell in love with your mother. You know the rest.'

'Do you mind talking about my grandmother? I never got to meet her.'

Walter drew in a long breath then continued.

'Hazel had missed out on seeing both you and Meg, as she died of complications of pneumonia during a hard winter when were snowed in. There was no time to get her to the hospital in Queenstown. I lived alone on Reed Station and isolated myself from the rest of the family after she'd gone.'

'That's so sad, Grandad. I wish I'd met her. But none of this was your fault.'

'I still think I need to make amends. I'll find a way to make it up to all of you. Just give me time.'

Large globules of water kept hanging on the end of the old man's nose. He pulled out a large wrinkled handkerchief and blew his nose like a foghorn.

Mack turned away and wiped his eyes with his sleeve.

'I suppose I should be getting back inside. Bessie rules me with an iron tongue sometimes.' He managed to laugh.

'Wait, Grandad.' Mack took his arm to stop him. He wrapped his arms around him. 'Thank so much for sharing all of this with me. I had no idea what you've suffered. You don't have to do it alone any longer.'

Walter squeezed his hand. 'You're not only a good shepherd, Mack. You're a top grandson. We're in this together.'

'I'd better start winding down too. I've got help some of our shepherds tomorrow to bring the sheep down to the woolshed. Shearing season has commenced.'

***

After he'd eaten his meal that night, Mack picked up the phone and called Jessie.

'I'm sorry I never got around to dropping off another load of firewood with my farm selling and everything. We've plenty of old pines up here so I can still do it in time for next winter if you remind me.'

Jessie leaned over her office desk rubbing her eyes and unwittingly yawned down the phone. 'Oops, sorry. I'm not bored, just really tired. Thanks for the offer. I'll put it in my diary for next autumn. I can come next Monday to do Zoro's vaccinations.'

'That suits me—but make it the afternoon if you can. Some contract shearers are coming tomorrow and they're leaving Monday morning. I need to sort out their wages before midday.'

'That'll be fine. See you Monday afternoon.'

Jessie was delighted. Perhaps she might get to spend a bit more time with Mack than she did with the last interrupted visit. Her social life was almost non-existent, and she had not yet made many friends in the area.

She went back into the kitchen to continue to prepare her meal. It was a fish pie she'd made from cans of smoked fish and mashed potatoes from her own vegetable garden.

She opened the oven door and checked that the breadcrumb topping had browned. It was ready to serve, and she'd developed a hearty appetite after a busy day running around the countryside in her car. The green peas on the cooktop were ready. As she picked up the spoon to serve her meal, the phone rang again. 'Oh, not now,' she uttered. She hurried back to her office and picked up the phone.

'Jessie, sorry to phone you at this time. I need to talk to you about something urgent that has cropped up.' It was Hope's father, Joel. There seemed to be an urgency in his voice. It sounded strained and croaky. Not his usual self.

'How about popping around tomorrow when you finish work— or another day if that doesn't suit?'

'Oh … okay. Is there a problem?' Jessie didn't usually get phone calls from Joel. She'd helped him out with foaling several times, but apart from that didn't visit his home that often. She would usually be with Hope and Cole for meals or babysitting for them.

'Not with me there isn't, but something has come up with some local farmers—look, let's not discuss it on the phone … dinner tomorrow?'

'If you don't mind, I won't stay for dinner. Need to do a heap of paperwork at home. I'll be over around five if that suits. It'll be a hectic schedule tomorrow on my clinic day at the surgery in Closeburn.'

Jessie put the phone back on the hook. Suddenly she'd lost her appetite. She didn't like the sound of Joel's voice. I had a negative tone that spelt trouble.

She'd been so hungry when she'd walked through the door after work but now the fish pie and green peas no longer held their appeal. Or was she worried for nothing? Instead of putting the food into the fridge until the next day, she served herself a small helping and forged her way through it after reheating it under the grill.

***

It had been a long and hot day with the inland temperatures around mid-twenties Celsius. Unusual for early December. Jessie had spent the morning with Robbie Byrnes assisting him with surgery on some of her own patients. She then had to drive up a long and dusty road towards Mount Judah to check the wound of a female dog she had spayed in the clinic the week before. The owner was elderly and make the trip to Closeburn.

I don't understand why people who don't drive, live remotely. They are so dependent on others.

The dog owner's neighbour dropped the dog off at the clinic on the day of the surgery and Jessie returned it to its owner after treatment.

The sheer stress of so much driving to patients in isolated areas and her weekly clinic in Closeburn exhausted her.

If only there was a clinic, she had access to in Glenorchy. She didn't have the finances to build one as she had plans to buy a home of her own.

There had to be another solution. It was easier for Max to manage when he was the remote vet, as he always had an extra colleague to help cover him until the last one resigned.

Vets in this area were as scarce as hen's teeth, especially experienced clinicians. Now Jessie was the only one north of Glenorchy and as far south as the Closeburn district. The trip took more than an hour on loose metal roads.

Perhaps she should raise the issue with Mack when she goes to give Zoro his vaccinations. Or even with Joel too.

Chapter Sixteen

Jessie loved driving down the long entrance to Dart River Ranch and to catch sight of Bertie toddling around the front garden. There was a wire fence between Hope and Cole's cottage and the large homestead that Hope's parents, Joel and Myra owned. But Cole had built an ornate, white picket fence around their humble home to keep Bertie safe. This time, Hope was on her front porch with Bertie. She waved out to her.

When she arrived at Joel's front door, Jessie knocked with trepidation, fearing what he was going to say. She couldn't guess what it was, but from the tremor in Joel's voice when he had spoken to her on the phone, she knew it wasn't good news.

Myra answered the door. 'Oh, Jessie—come on in. Joel isn't far away. He has been expecting you. I'll go out back and call him.'

She ushered Jessie into the lounge and then went back into the kitchen to put the kettle on.

Jessie sank into the armchair and sat plucking at the fluff on her shirt-blouse. Nervously she started twirling a strand of her sandy coloured hair with her index finger then sat tugging on it. The house cat spotted her and must have sensed her lack of composure. It started rubbing its soft coat along her shins, giving her a degree of comfort.

'Jessie, good to see you. Glad you were able to come at such short notice. I know how busy you are.' Joel stood there looking more serious than usual giving her a half-smile.

'Not as busy as I'd like to be. At least, not in these parts—I haven't been getting as many calls from the Vet Co-op the past few weeks. I really thought by now that business would be thriving, seeing that I'm the only remote vet in the area.'

Joel gave a nervous cough. He didn't sit down this time.

'Look—I think it might be better if we go into my office if you don't mind. We have a few ranch hands working close to the house today. They often use the bathroom and I'd rather give you some privacy.'

Jessie followed him into the office while Myra hovered around offering them some refreshments.

'If you don't mind, just a glass of water would be fine, thanks.' Jessie smiled at Myra who brought in a jug of water and glasses. Joel closed the door after her.

Joel had been like a second father to Jessie since she had moved down South. He was always jovial around her and had given her much encouragement whenever she was treating his animals. This was the first time she had been ill at ease with him—or perhaps she was just over-reacting.

He sat back in his seat, crossing his feet and clasping his hands together on his lap.

'Well, Jessie, I don't know how to broach this issue as I believe you're going to find it distressing, but please bear with me and don't for a moment think that I agree with any of it,' he spouted.

Jessie's muscles in her jaw tensed. A surge of adrenaline raced around her body as she prepared herself for the worst.

'I have just attended the committee meeting of the High Country Farmers Association. We meet quarterly and this week's meeting was a real eye-opener. They had been discussing the new remote vet, namely you, and what they had to say was not awe-inspiring, to say the least.'

'Oh no! What do you mean?' Jessie's forehead puckered as she started biting her lip.

'There are some hot-heads amongst them, mostly farmers who have been in the area for decades and who hold prejudice against female professionals like you, no matter how clever or skilled you are. In fact, I was so offended by their behaviour and the derogatory way they spoke about you, I almost walked out. But instead, I stayed till the end to defend you.'

'That is so mean. What have I done to deserve all this? Please—be honest with me, Joel.'

'I am being honest. The thing is, in the end not one of them was able to make an incriminating report about your professional or clinical conduct. It all stemmed from an absolute abhorrence of any females working in the capacity of a vet in any situation. A lot of these farmers see women as domestics, either hanging out nappies on the clothesline or cooking the meals for their station hands. Occasionally some of their wives work on the farms with them but it is not that common. They are there to back up the men in a domestic capacity. But that's not how folks brought me up on the farm.'

'Nor was it like that on my parents' farm. My mother and I used to round up the sheep and cattle along with my brother so we didn't need to hire farmhands. Sometimes we employed a house-keeper at a particularly busy time but my mother was not a doormat.'

'Well then—these men will have to learn a few home truths. We need to find a way for you to show them you can match the skill of any vet between here and Queenstown, including Max. I know your worth and they need to know too.'

'But if the whole province is against me, how can I succeed? Anyway, who are these men, this vigilante? Please, Joel—just tell me who the ring leader is and I'll avoid them.'

She gulped down half a glass of water then cringed as she realised how loud it sounded—indicating her agitation.

'I think it's a case of them avoiding you and telling the Co-op to send them another vet. They have to pay the extra travel expenses that the other vets will charge though so it's a case of the "cutting off the nose to spite the face".'

'Who is the one who has instigated it? Is it old Mr Greeson? He was pretty grumpy last week when I visited his farm. He had half a dozen cows I had to take serum samples from and he was so negative, complaining about all his neighbours including me. He wasn't even interested in holding the animals still to help me do my job properly. I was glad to leave there.'

'No ... it was that Scotsman McKlintoch on the deer farm. He was the main one stirring the pot. He has a real big chip on his shoulder.'

'Of course, I should have known. He was that unpleasant man who yelled at me and gave me a few really nasty looks.'

'Everyone around here knows he is Master of the Hunts. He thinks he's a cut above the rest of the community because of the first-rate horses he bred.'

'What am I to do? This is my livelihood. He might turn them all against me. Perhaps I should move.' She drooped, placing her elbows on her thighs and resting her face in her hands. Her head was thumping as though it was about to explode. She was sure her blood pressure had risen.

Joel saw the deflated look on her face. It was obvious it exasperated her. 'No—don't think like that. You mustn't take on board their rubbish. They are just blowing hot wind. You must detach and I'll get my buddies in the area to bring you influence.'

'I don't know. It will be hard to believe I will ever break into this community.' All Jessie wanted was her own father to pray for her just as he used to when she was still living at home. She found it hard to lift her head as though they had drained her life force from her.

'Jessie.' She looked up, responding to Joel's gentle voice.

'Let me pray for you and ask God for guidance in this situation. In fact, I'd like to ask for a breakthrough in such a way that this community of farmers will not only accept you but also honour you as a clinician in your own right.'

'Oh ... okay then, thanks.' She bowed her head as Joel prayed an articulated prayer that seemed to emulate her father when he used to pray for her. It made her relax and her confidence returned. She turned to Joel with a heart full of appreciation. This time she could smile without forcing it and Joel's sympathetic facial expression had sufficient warmth to soothe her soul.

Chapter Seventeen

Jessie arrived home from her visit with Joel, off-loaded her bags in her office, and crashed on her bed. She didn't bother to remove her boots, as she was drained—still upset from the negative feedback she'd received from him, even though he told her to ignore it.

The attack on her personal and professional reputation had left her reeling. She'd worked hard at building up her credibility in this remote, rural community and had done everything possible to become integrated, but it had been futile. What chance did she have now of building up her veterinarian practice with this vigilante mentality determined to undermine and discredit her? In spite of what Joel, Cole, Mack, and even Walter Reed had said in her favour, she'd begun to lose confidence in herself.

Right now she wished she had her little cat from back home to comfort her. The fat, fluffy, ginger animal always knew when she was hurting, and at times like this, she would bury her face in the cat's long bushy fur until it had soaked up her warm tears. But this time, there was no furry comforter, just her eiderdown saturated by the continual flow of droplets as she sobbed her heart out.

She spoke out loud to her creator—*'that's it, God. You said that you would be my comforter and protector but I can't take much more of this. I've decided that, if I encounter one more case of bullying from those mean-spirited farmers, I'll toss the towel in and head back to the Waikato to do a job without my heart being in it, just going through the motions—if that's what you want me to do, God, I will.'*

Later, having slept a little, she awoke glad to be home after the long intense session with Joel. She sat at her dining table staring at the walls wondering if her dream of being a high country vet had now been shattered. She was exhausted from all the pent-up emotion and hardly had the energy to get up and prepare a meal. She'd completely lost her appetite. Suddenly floods of tears soaked the tablecloth where she sat sobbing her heart out again. How can she go on like this? Perhaps she had made the wrong decision about taking the role of a remote vet—or any kind of vet in this area, for that matter. She roughly blew her nose and tried to compose herself so she could think. She wondered if she'd misheard God speaking to her heart in her prayers when she was back in the Waikato and had prayed hard for guidance before she took the job on. What a mess. Perhaps she should talk to Mack about it. He might be able to help her shed some light on the unpleasant predicament in which she had landed herself.

Her heart was almost breaking at the thought of having to give it all up—the mountains, the lakes, as well as her best friend, Hope. Of course, there were other friends such as Mack too. She suddenly remembered she was due to visit him the next day but first had to visit a sick animal not far from her house—a miniature horse that was lame. The farmers were kind people and the last time she had visited them they had treated Jessie with respect. The woman had even given her a brown paper bag full of freshly baked muffins. Tomorrow will be a relaxing day she decided, as she ran a bath full of bubbles.

***

The next day the visit with the elderly couple was a complete change from dealing with the handful of obnoxious farmers in the area. These humble people who bred tiny horses were a breeze. They fussed over Jessie and esteemed her highly. This time they invited her to stay for lunch after she'd taken care of the horse.

103

The cute animal was lame from a deep bruise which Jessie ascertained had been caused by the last dumping of snow in the spring. Its hoof had probably become impacted with ice, she had told them. Because the horse had no shoes, the bruise had become worse while trotting on the stony tracks around the farm when the grandchildren came to ride him.

'It will need rest, and once the swelling has gone down I'll check it again to see if he is ready to be shod. The shoes will protect his feet.'

After a pleasant lunch, Jessie said farewell and zoomed back onto the main highway heading towards Reed Station. She began rehearsing what she wanted to tell Mack. As she veered around the tight corners, a hare shot out under the vehicle which swerved, skidding several metres on the loose metal. It came to a halt in the long grass at the side of the road. Her hands, still glued to the wheel were shaking. She gasped. The impact had forced the air from her lungs. Relieved to discover she'd avoid hitting the animal that had skittled into the bushes she knew it was wrong to swerve to avoid them.

Ten minutes later she'd regained her composure and managed to drive her vehicle out of the long grass and back onto the road.

What a day, she thought. She hoped nothing else would go wrong for the rest of the week. It was a welcome sight to see the attractive colonial homestead belonging to Walter Reed but now Mack Reed lived there too which made it even more inviting.

She drove into her usual parking area at the side of the house and was greeted by Mack's border collie, Bluey. He stood next to the vehicle greeting her with a friendly yelp as she rolled down her window to say hello, the dog placed his paws on the window ledge.

'Get out of there,' called Mack. 'Sorry about that. He knows better than to do that.' He walked forward and helped her inside with her bag.

'Have you got time to come inside for a cool drink first? Bessie has just opened a new batch of ginger beer, her special recipe.'

'Ah ... sure. Thanks, I'd love to.'

They sat at the dining table and drank the ice-cold, invigorating beverage while they caught up on all their news. While Bessie loomed in the background, Jessie was not yet ready to tell Mack her sad story about her rebuff from the anti-female-vet brigade, she called them.

After their short catch up on all the latest local news, Mack carried her bag as they wandered over to the stable where he had penned Zoro.

'You know he's a very special horse, Mack, especially after the incident with your grandfather. He appears to have extrasensory perception or something. Either that or he is exceptionally intelligent. Perhaps he can be used to help others to heal someday. It's worth thinking about.'

'I like that phrase you used—extra what? Anyway, I think he has that.' They both chuckled as they entered Zoro's pen.

After she gave the horse a full examination to check his fitness for the shots, Jessie administered the vaccinations. Later on, Mack invited her to sit on the veranda for a rest to recover from her incident with the hare that she'd reported to him.

As they both sat on the bench staring out at the acres of paddocks on the horizon, Mack asked her how she'd been doing since her last visit and whether the business had started to build up.

'I've been referring my mates to you through the Vet Co-op, so hopefully, that might help.'

'Thanks, Mack. I really appreciate it. Most of them tell me if you have referred them to me. They are the decent ones worth having on my books. Not like some of them.'

'Oh that's good—but what do you mean? Are you getting some unpleasant clients out here?'

'Unpleasant is too kind a word for certain farmers around here. I would say outright nasty, in fact.'

She couldn't withhold it any longer and just caved in. She squeezed her eyes to try to hold back the unwanted tears, but they started to slide down her face, the salt stinging the cracks in her dry lips. She tried hard not to sob heavily but her emotions threatened her.

'Oh, no, what's happened. Who has upset you? Tell me, Jessie. What's been going on and maybe I can help.' He placed his arm across her shoulders then pulled back, not knowing what her reaction would be.

'I've noticed that a bunch of local high country farmers have intentionally not requested my services, in fact, not for months. The usual clients on Max's books have not wanted me to visit their farms.'

'Perhaps they've had no need for a vet for some time.'

'No, that's not true. They have deliberately been avoiding me, Joel Grey told me yesterday. They discussed my plight at the recent meeting of the High Country Farmers Association and several of them were caustic about having to put up with a female vet. Joel said they had not one bit of evidence to back up their argument and he fought for my defence.'

'Ridiculous old fools,' Mack snorted. 'Who on earth do they think they are? Those men are just deeply entrenched in narrow-mindedness and prejudice and haven't moved on—and times are changing.'

'But that doesn't mean they have to be nasty and unwelcoming. No one can change them after all these years and I'm afraid they will turn more and more farmers against me.' She sniffed loudly then blew her nose just as noisily on her handkerchief. Mack handed her another glass of ginger beer that Bessie had put out on the veranda earlier for them.

'I think maybe I might have to move away. It's just too hard managing this whole area by myself, driving miles each day along rough, windy, and dusty roads to ungrateful bigoted men who despise me.'

'Would you like me to pray with you? I don't mind, honest.'

'That's okay, don't worry. Joel prayed with me yesterday. I just needed to offload it.'

'It sounds like a regular case of bullying too. Look, Jessie, let me tell you about a similar experience I had as a young lad starting out on farms. That's when I first worked as a sheep shearing contractor. I was not your run-of-the-mill, beer-swilling, rugby-mad contractor like many of them. I was a shy, sensitive guy back then and kept to myself a lot. I was ostracised for not drinking or hanging around the girls in bars. They used to single me out and often start a fight with me just for the fun of it. Some bullies would even take credit for the sheep I had sheared.'

Jessie went quiet. For the first time, she was able to see Mack's soul, his real self.

Mack continues, 'I toughened up and learned how to box and even learnt some martial arts. I also went to a sheep shearing expert to learn great skills that won me awards. The worst thing was that some of them were abusing the sheep—badly. So much that some poor animals had broken eye sockets and head injuries from being kicked or battered with tools. A few of the shearers even stole wool or the odd sheep and sold them on the side. I became a *whistle-blower.'*

It sickened Jessie to listen to this, but he was drawing an analogy to what was happening to her.

'Men in positions of power abusing weaker, vulnerable ones,' she uttered. Her eyes widened, and she fixed her gaze on Mack's face as he continued with his story.

'One bloke deliberately provoked and picked a fight with me. He came off second best. That was the last time they ever went near me. I didn't run from it. You have to show them you aren't afraid. I've heard stories of excellence about your work, Jessie, so never doubt yourself.'

Jessie was speechless. She admired Mack for sharing something so personal and just sat still, soaking up every word.

'Look, Jessie. I want to share a verse from the Bible with you that changed my perception of the situation, a scripture that gave me hope and courage and made me realise that God understands. It goes like this ...

This is what the Sovereign Lord says: 'Should not shepherds take care of the flock? You eat the curds, clothe yourselves with the wool, and slaughter the choice animals, but you do not take

*care of the flock. You have not strengthened the weak or healed
the sick or bound up the injured. You have not brought back the
strays or searched for the lost. You have ruled them harshly and
brutally. I am against the shepherds and will hold them
accountable for my flock. I will remove them from tending the
flock so that the shepherds can no longer feed themselves. I will
rescue my flock from their mouths, and it will no longer be food
for them. For this is what the Sovereign Lord says; I myself will
search for my sheep and look after them. As a shepherd looks
after his scattered flock when he is with them, so will I look after
my sheep. I will rescue them from all the places where they were
scattered on a day of clouds and darkness.'*

Jessie had not heard Mack speak like this before. She was
speechless after he spoke those words from the Bible, trembling
from head to toe.

'How are you finding the workload at present?' Mack asked.

She composed herself. 'The Co-op should have replaced the
other vet who had shared the province with Max. Now Max has
gone that just leaves me. I mean ... they haven't even provided me
with a clinic.'

'There has never been a clinic here, but we've certainly needed
one.'

'I read about those mobile surgical units in the United States
and even Australia that they use in remote areas like this. Perhaps
I need to try that as one last solution to the problem. I've been
thinking—instead of buying myself a house of my own, I could
purchase a small bus and turn it into a mobile, fully functioning
clinic. Then many of the clients with smaller animals can bring
them to me. I'll also be able to carry out minor surgery in it instead
of having to travel all the way into the one near Closeburn. If that
doesn't work out, I'll just have to pack up and head back to the
Waikato, as my old boss will give me my job back again any time.
What do you think?'

Mack's face dropped. Suddenly his countenance took on a
sombre serious expression. He scratched his head and started
blinking nervously.

'Oh, Jessie. I'm sure it won't come to that. I do rather like the idea of the mobile clinic but not having to forfeit being able to have your own home. I know how hard you'd been saving for that. And those pompous fools at that meeting ... I believe Max had about fifty high country farmers on his books and there is only a handful who are behaving badly. You continue to prove your worth as you have been and they'll fade into insignificance. You mark my words.'

Jessie wasn't convinced but trusted Mack's opinion. She was a lot happier now that she'd offloaded it.

A truck roared down the driveway and came to a halt in front of the house. It was Walter who had been driving and appeared to have had a full recovery from his minor stroke.

'That's a surprise to see Walter driving already. Is he okay now?'

'He's fine. No trouble with his legs, just one arm is a little weak and his speech slightly slower, but the doctor said he will probably completely recover. He is looking forward to seeing you. By the way—I forgot to tell you that Grandad, and I have reconciled and forgiven each other. He seems to be a changed man and comes to home church with me now and then.'

Jessie's heart leapt. It was amazing news, something that really uplifted her.

'In fact, he wants to invite my family to share Christmas with us and he suggested that you might like to come too, seeing you saved his life, he told me. What do you think?'

Jessie couldn't believe her ears. She was on a roller coaster ride with so many emotional ups and downs and a boost.

'I'd love to—oh, hi there,' she addressed Walter who walked towards her with his face beaming, showing a whole set of new dentures after the last set had been broken during his fall.

'What a nice surprise to see you, Jessie. In fact, I think I owe you for saving my life out there in the field that day.' He put out his hand and shook hers, hesitating before he released it. 'It seems that I am in your debt.'

Her face flushed. She wasn't used to such flattery.

'Oh, it wasn't me who rescued you, it was Zoro. You'd been lying flat on your back when I arrived and had been covered with hay. I guess Zoro had scattered it over you to keep the cold out.'

'You're right. The last thing I remember was carrying a small bale of hay into the paddock, but that would have been where the gate is, a long way from where I fell. He's an unusual champion, that stallion, unlike any I've ever seen—but you ran to my aid I hear and got help.' He turned to Mack. 'I hope you talked to her about Christmas. It's only a few weeks away.'

'Yes, Grandad, she's coming.'

Walter walked off into the kitchen and the wry grin stayed on his face while he handed Bessie the groceries he had brought back from the General Store.

Jessie drove off down the driveway back onto the main road, and her smile never left her face until she arrived home.

Chapter Eighteen

After a hectic day and her visit with Mack and Walter, Jessie's feet ached. Her toes burned inside her new leather boots that threatened to blister her tender feet. She sat up and tugged at them until they dropped onto the floor then sat staring out of the window. She was trying to remember the scripture that Mack had so eloquently poured forth to give her encouragement. She picked up her Bible and found the verse which she read out loud. Then it came to her—just as Mack had responded to his bullies, she would become bold too. God was on her side and he would give her the inspiration and help she needed to come out on top.

She was startled by the phone ringing in her office. She didn't want to answer it as she'd planned to start reading the new C. S. Lewis novel she'd brought home from the tiny Glenorchy library the week before, but she was on call for the next twenty-four hours. She answered with a flat tone in her voice. It was the Vet Call Centre.

'Who? McKlintoch you say, from Priory Road? I didn't think he wanted me to go back there. He doesn't like female vets. Can't you ask one of the vets in Closeburn or Queenstown?' Jessie raised the tone of her voice, vehemently opposed to going to his farm.

'I have tried everywhere. There are vets off sick with the bug that's going around and some are away on holiday. You appear to be the only one left. One of Doug's best hinds has gone into labour and needs help urgently.'

Oh yes, that has to happen to me of all people. He doesn't deserve my help. She wanted to explain the situation about his bullying but knew it would sound strange over the phone.

'He said the hind is having twins and has some complications. You are the only one left to help.'

'Are you sure he said, twins? It's very unusual for red deer to have twins.' Jessie's heart sank even further.

'He certainly said that, and he asked for someone who is skilled in delivering them. I said you had safely assisted many cattle, horses, sheep, even twins during birth, but not deer. I told him not to worry as deer usually give birth unaided in the wild.'

'Please let him know that it will be me attending the birth. I'm sure he'll refuse.'

'I've already told him you are his only option. You don't have to rush as she has only just gone into true labour, he said.'

Jessie knew she's been bludgeoned into agreeing to go and help her enemy as she saw him. But deep down, she figured that somehow this might be the way to win this man's admiration. On the other hand, if it all turned to custard, she would abandon ship and leave the beautiful south—heartbroken, of course.

***

She wound her way along the rough, loose metal road to the deer farm. She saw a logging truck pelting towards her. In an instant, she swerved to the side into the long grass to let him pass —CRACK! A large stone shattered her windscreen. 'Stupid fool!', she yelled as she stepped out of her vehicle, almost in tears. She went around to the back of the vehicle and took out a dustpan and brush to clear the shattered glass away from the inside of the car and placed it in a paper bag she had in her glove-box. If only she'd noted his licence plate number but was too shaken up. She had a much more important agenda.

This was one of the drawbacks of living in Glenorchy. She had to get used to the potholes and stony roads. No lovely tar-seal, like some parts of Queenstown.

Shaken up and discouraged, she stepped back into the vehicle and made her way up to McKlintoch's farm.

Doug McKlintoch paced up and down the path in front of his house waiting for Jessie as her vehicle swerved into the driveway and screeched to a halt, almost knocking him over. Bad start, she thought. She scrambled out of the vehicle almost falling over and pulled her medical bag off the back seat.

Doug, over six foot high, stood erect—his form looming over her, far too close for her liking. She got a whiff of the perspiration that ran down his tomato coloured temples and dripped off the end of his nose.

'Hurry, woman! I don't know what to do with her. I'm at my wit's end and I don't want to lose her. She's my prize breeder—you'd better get this right!'

'Sorry—I got a stone in my windscreen and it shattered.'

'Is that right? Let's get this job done first and we'll worry about that later.'

He panted his way along the track with Jessie in close pursuit to the barn where the hind was still on her feet. Jessie kept thinking of the difficult twin births she'd assisted with her father's cattle and although she'd never attended the birth of twin red deer, she'd gained plenty of experience and confidence with birthing farm animals. Though she'd never had a bully standing over her intimidating her.

She placed her medical bag on the thick layer of hay in the corner of the pen. Doug was still panicking and started to annoy her.

'Can't you see she's in trouble? Hurry up and do something! She's been pacing up and down for an hour now.'

With that, she looked him in the eye as close as possible and spoke firmly. 'Look here, Doug ... I'm an experienced vet and have successfully delivered twin calves and breeches, some of them from large Highland cattle. Do you think the Vet Co-op would have employed me as a remote vet to high country farm animals if I was incompetent? Either you put your trust in me and let me do my job without harassing me, or I'll walk away right now!'

The sharpness of her tone and the accompanying threat was enough to cause him to teeter backwards. He slumped down onto a stack of feed that lay at one side of the pen and wiped away the sweat from his brow with his sleeve.

'Right you are,' he stammered. 'I'll leave you to it, lass. Let me know if you need anything.' He pointed to a steel bucket of hot water and a bottle of disinfectant for her to clean her hands and arms. A clean towel lay next to it. After scrubbing up, Jessie donned her long rubber gloves and examined the animal. A few minutes later she reassured the nervous farmer.

'I think this fine mother is going to do quite well without too much intervention. I'll just stand by and give her a helping hand when necessary. She's in normal labour but with twins, it's going to take a while. It's incredibly uncomfortable because of the pressure of the two babies, and that's why she's pacing up and down to relieve it—not because she's having complications.'

'Is that right? So where's she at then?'

'I'll have to help her along gently, but we should start seeing the hooves and head of the first one soon, by the look of her. But I may need to give her some assistance with the second one. They can be a little tricky.'

'Thanks for that. I'll slip inside to ask my wife, Jill if she'd make you a cup of tea.'

'Thanks, I'd love one.' Jessie let out a deep breath of relief to have him out of her presence briefly.

His prickly demeanour had changed to one of angst. He hurried inside the house and called out to his wife Jill who, in a short time brought them a tray of tea and chocolate biscuits. She placed it on a shelf near the action and walked away quietly and left them to it.

Contrary to Doug's overreaction and incorrect presumptions, the hind experienced no great complications except that the birth of the second one took longer than the first.

By eight o'clock that night, the second of her two healthy calves had been born. Jessie had eased it out of the birth canal and Doug placed it where its mother could reach it to start cleaning it and bonding. Both the twins had both arrived safely.

Doug and Jessie left the hind in peace to continue bonding with her twins and wandered over to the house. Jessie was exhausted from the build-up of nervous tension and the farmer's face was as white as a sheet.

He wouldn't stop thanking and praising her. 'You don't know how grateful I am that you came out here. No one else would come, and the Call Centre told me you were quite reluctant because I'd caused you so much grief recently.'

Jessie just nodded and said nothing, still shaking from all the stress of the challenging day she'd had.

'I know it's late, but please come inside. Jill has kept some supper for you, as she knew it would be a long night. Please, Jessie. I need to talk to you before you go and then I'll take a look at that windscreen.'

Was this the breakthrough she'd hoped for? Perhaps he really was human after all. Anyway—she'd worked up quite an appetite and her stomach was screeching out for food.

'Oh, thanks, I will. Have you some clean water for me to wash up with?'

He ushered her to the outside laundry where she could clean up properly. While she was out there, she heard Doug through the kitchen window on the phone to one of his colleagues saying how great the new vet was and what a wonderful job she'd done with assisting the delivery of the twin fawns. Jessie knew that the word would spread and at last she would be able to relax. She silently thanked God.

When she sat at the table eating the beef hot pot and drinking hot chocolate, Jill made her feel welcome by inviting her to be a guest speaker at the Country Women's Institute meeting in the new year. By the end of the evening, Jessie knew that they would become friends.

While Jill was busy in the kitchen with the dishes, Doug sat in the lounge with Jessie, trying to make amends.

'Look—I know I've been a thorn in your side and have misjudged you ... I'm sorry for all the trouble I caused when I hardly knew anything about you. I realise there's no excuse for my bad behaviour, but many of us old boys on the farms out here have lived on our family farms for generations. We've never had female vets, let alone women managing farms. But I realise now we'll just have to adjust to changing times, and you have proved to be a pioneer in your own right, Jessie. Please forgive me for the pain I have brought into your life. I'll be telling a different story to the committee of High Country Farmers—in fact, I'll draft a letter to them tomorrow.'

Jessie didn't know what to say. She was moved by his confession and just managed to utter, 'Thank you for trusting me. I'd better get on the road now.'

'Wait, a moment—I have something in my shed that might make do until you can get your windscreen fixed.' He turned the light on in the shed and had to wade through a lot of stored items to find a windscreen cover. Eventually, he brought it back onto the porch to show Jessie.

'What do you think of this?' he asked, wiping the dust off with a cloth.

'Oh, that's superb. I've never seen one of these before.'

'Good, let me take a look at it. Hop into your vehicle and drive it closer to the porch to catch the light.'

Jessie did what he said, and in less than half an hour he had the plastic cover firmly in place. Jessie was over the moon, and instead of seeing him as her enemy, her perception of him had rapidly changed into a gentle giant towering over her.

'I hope you have full car insurance, as they usually cover broken windscreens and you certainly need it out here.'

'Yes, I was advised about it by Max before he left. It's all taken care of, thanks again. I am so grateful for your help. Let me know how the twins get along, and if you have any problems, please phone the Call Centre to get me out here as soon as you can.'

She poked her head into the kitchen. 'Bye, Jill. Please let me know when you want me to do that speaking engagement. I'm off now.'

Doug and Jill waved her off from their porch as she tooted, driving out onto the highway into the dark abyss with the security of her radio-phone hanging on the dashboard. No lights for miles except for the bright headlights of her vehicle and the wide eyes of the odd opossum that stopped momentarily on the road then shot to the side as she passed. She barely believed what had taken place—but tonight was the beginning of a whole new exciting chapter of her life. Only a week ago she had thought she may not have been mentally strong enough for this demanding and challenging work out in the middle of nowhere. But God did for her what she was not able to do for herself. And now it was evident that she wouldn't have to leave the mountains and her friends whom she held dear. She was here to stay.

But for now, she had to contact Mack's mechanic to book her windscreen in for repair. He had been able to get her a good discount with this mechanic. Although it was unlikely, she would try to get it fixed through New Year.

Right now she had greater fish to fry and Mack was her priority at this time.

Chapter Nineteen

Jessie stood in the mirror tying then retying her lilac scarf. She wanted to wear it with her white short-sleeved cotton jumper and mauve skirt, but the way she draped the scarf around her neck just didn't look right. She hung it back up in the wardrobe then walked over to her dresser, lifting the lid of her cherished wooden jewellery box that played the tune of *The Sugar Plum Fairy*. One by one she sifted through the pile of necklaces to find one that suited her outfit.

'Ah—here it is, just the right one,' she uttered, standing back in front of the mirror, struggling with the clasp on the necklace of synthetic amethysts. They contrasted well with her mauve skirt and blue eyes.

The necklace had sentimental value, as her parents had given it to her for her twenty-first birthday and she had always cherished it.

She was a little guilty that this would be the first Christmas that she hadn't spent at home with her folks, even though she had promised them instead that she would see the New Year in with them and her brother. She had planned to stay for a week if the Vet Co-op could get someone to fill in for her.

Mack insisted Jessie arrive early on Christmas Day so she would be able to meet his family before Christmas lunch. She had some trepidation about being in the middle of strained family relations, and even if Walter was willing to forgive and forget the past, the family may not be so full of grace. Nevertheless, she was a guest of Mack's and would support him through it as a loyal friend.

***

Mack's border collie, Bluey was the only farm dog that was allowed to run around the house. He was treated as one of the family, as he had been more than a working dog. He was to Mack, a beloved friend. Mack had always let him inside the house, although at Walter's place he had to stay outside at night and sleep on the veranda. He had his own special kennel outside Mack's bedroom door that led onto the long, wooden deck. Unbeknown to Walter, now and then during the winter, Mack would sneak him into his bedroom to sleep on his mat—only when Bessie was away visiting her family, as she would *blow the whistle* on him if she knew. The other farm dogs were in warm kennels several metres away from the farmhouse.

As Jessie drove up to the house, Bluey ran out to greet her as usual but knew not to jump up on her vehicle. She glanced around at the two strange cars in the driveway and guessed they must belong to Mack's family. She sat with the engine running, not knowing where to park. She didn't want to park far from the house as she had a large Pavlova with cream sitting on the seat next to her in a plastic cake carrier and imagined herself tripping and sending the thing flying, or worse still, smashing it down the front of her skirt.

Mack caught sight of her and rushed forward, waving at her.

'Hold on!' he called as she wound her window down. 'Over here, next to the house. I'll shift the quad bike.'

He jumped on the bike and moved it away from the house.

'Sorry, I should have moved it a lot earlier to make way for all the vehicles.'

She stepped out and went to the passenger door to reach for the Pavlova.

'Here—let me help you with that. It sure looks good. The family have come with cakes, but no one has brought one of these. Christmas isn't the same without one.'

'The strawberries are from my garden, by the way.'

119

'Ah, yes. Hope and Cole told me you've got green fingers. Come inside and meet my family.'

Jessie tried to ignore the hard knot forming inside her stomach and the tension in the back of her neck, as he said that. She followed behind him into the kitchen, as he placed the Pavlova on the sideboard.

'Let me pour you a drink before we go into the lounge. The family is all in there. Some have brought wine, and I made a large punchbowl. I've also got Bessie's ginger beer in the fridge.'

'Punch would be fine, thanks.'

'I'll tell you all about the new relationship my grandfather has with my family. It's a miracle. Thanks for your prayers, by the way. Let's talk later on. They arrived yesterday evening, and after lunch today, Grandad is taking them on a tour of the station.'

They carried their beverages into the lounge where there appeared to be a congenial atmosphere, much to Jessie's surprise after all the negativity she'd heard.

Mack's parents, Len and Helen stood up out of their chairs, as Jessie entered the room, followed by his sister, Meg and her husband, Joe, which unnerved her. She loathed being the focus of attention, as they moved forward to shake her hand.

'Well—we finally get to meet you,' said Helen softly, giving Jessie the sweetest smile. Jessie was taken in by the warmth of her eyes. She would easily take a liking to her. Len, who had given her a hard handshake, almost too hard for her liking, had sharp features and appeared to be a typical detached businessman in his manner— far removed from Mack who seemed to take after his mother, even in appearance with her thick, wavy hair and high cheekbones.

Jessie was overcome by the pressure of suddenly having to relate to Mack's family all at once. They bombarded her with questions about her vet role in a remote area. The women couldn't take their eyes off her.

Meg went with her mother to organise the dishes to go on the table. Walter sat in the corner chatting to Jessie about the favourable feedback he'd heard from his farming friends about the way she'd assisted Doug McKlintoch's prized hind deer giving birth to twins. Mack caught up with his brother-in-law, telling him about the successful working merino sheep station he now managed.

Walter had given Bessie a few days off while his family were staying. She'd gone to stay with her own family in Cromwell.

'Mack, would you mind slicing the ham and turkey for us,' Meg asked, nodding at Mack. He raced into the kitchen like an obedient child and after slicing the ham, took it into the dining room, and placed it on the table as Meg directed him. 'Joe, please can you bring in the turkey, please? It'll need cutting up too.'

Jessie's eyes almost stood out on stalks as she saw the size of the enormous turkey.

'Grandad, would you mind blessing the food for us, please?' asked Mack, while Len and Helen looked at them both somewhat taken aback. As Walter prayed and gave thanks for the food, he also thanked God for the restoration of his family. Then surprisingly for Mack, his father joined in and gave thanks for Walter and Mack and all that God was doing in healing their relationships. Helen followed suit too, but Joe and Meg remained quiet, appearing a little embarrassed. Jessie gathered that the rest of the family had accepted God into their lives but perhaps Joe and Meg weren't quite there yet. She and Mack would have to keep praying for them.

Christmas lunch was a joyful occasion as Jessie carefully observed the interaction between Mack and each member of his family. She liked the way that he appeared to thrive in a family setting—just as she had done with her own family back in Bethlehem. After they rested, the guests all decided to walk off the first course. They saved Jessie's Pavlova, Meg's cheesecake and Mack's fresh fruit salad for later on. Walter offered to take the family on a tour of the station in his truck.

***

Jessie and Mack were busy in the kitchen putting the dishes away after the main meal, while Mack's family readied themselves to go on the farm tour.

'They'll be at least an hour or longer doing that tour with Grandad. That's how long it'll take to show them all the farming operations. Let's go for a walk down by the river? It's going to be a warm afternoon so we'll get a pleasant cool breeze off the water.'

Jessie looked at her shoes which were unsuitable for stumbling over animal dung and rough ground.

'Oh ... I'd love to, but I didn't bring my walking shoes, sorry.'

'Ah, no need to worry. We can just sit out on the veranda until they come back. I should have phoned you to ask you to bring them.'

Jessie rolled her eyes and banged her hand down on the bench, annoyed with herself that she'd removed the spare boots from her vehicle that she usually carried with her. She had taken them out to clean them and forgotten to put them back.

'Are you okay—what's wrong?'

'Just annoyed that I haven't got my spare boots in my Land Rover. I'd love to come for a walk along the river.'

Mack placed the baking dish he was holding back onto the oven top and grabbed her arm. 'Wait here a minute ... what size are your boots?'

'Size eight. Woman's size, that is.'

Mack raced down the other end of the house where his family were staying and called out to his sister. He explained the situation to Meg, and she handed him a pair of trainers. He hurried back to Jessie. 'Here, try these on, I think they should fit. She and Joe are going to take my Ute and follow the others on tour.'

The shoes fitted perfectly. 'Come on, let's go. Make the most of the time they are away. They're taking off now.'

The water level of the river was still high, even in December, as there had been a few random dumps of snow the last few nights. The water was a beautiful turquoise, full of glacial flour—the fine-grained silt that created the colour.

'I love seeing this. You only see it in the south. It's gorgeous,' Jessie said as she stood staring at the water.

At the side of the river was a small group of apple trees with ripe fruit. Mack reached up above his head and plucked a red apple and handed it to Jessie.

'Try this—it's one of Grandad's prize varieties that has been in the family for generations. It's crisp and sweet.'

Jessie started munching on the fruit then picked another one, slipping it into her pocket.

'Come! I want to show you an amazing view.' They kept walking alongside the river until Mack stopped to point to something standing in the clearing by the pine trees. It was a horse—a beautiful golden Palomino watching them from a distance. It whinnied softly.

'Wow! Where did you get that? It's gorgeous ... a mare, isn't it?' Jessie pushed a branch of an overhanging young poplar tree aside to get a better look.

'She is your Christmas present. I had my eye on her when I saw her amongst Joel Grey's herd and asked him to keep her for you. I saved up and paid Joel off while I was still on my own farm. I waited until you had purchased your own grazing as you had planned, but you can graze her here for now.' Mack's smile stretched across his face as he looked back at Jessie and saw her eyes were full of tears—tears of joy. She turned and wrapped her arms around him squeezing him tight. 'How did you know I wanted one so badly?'

'Hope told me you had to leave your own horse, Rusty behind and how heart-broken you were. I put her in this paddock so that you wouldn't see her from the house, but she can't stay in here and demolish all Grandad's apples.'

'But what about Walter? What does he think about me grazing her on the farm?'

'I think he might not be too fussed when he hears about the second gift I have for you,' he said with smiling eyes.

'Oh, no, I haven't given you yours yet? It's in my Land Rover. I didn't want to do it in front of everyone today. I planned to give it to you before I went home.' Jessie turned to look at Mack, and for an instant, he had left the spot where he was standing. She watched him stoop down to the ground as if he was searching for something.

'Ah, here it is!' He had dropped something in the grass and his face had turned the colour of beetroot. Jessie approached him.

'What was it you dropped?'

He stayed on his knees.

'Are you okay, why don't you get up?'

'I dropped your other gift—well, actually it's not really a gift, it's a ... goodness, Jessie will you marry me?' he managed to blurt out, trying to remain upright kneeling on one leg on the rough, uneven ground.

Jessie stood stunned, her mouth and eyes wide open as if she couldn't believe what she had just heard.

'Yes, yes, of course, I will!'

He managed to pull the sparkling diamond ring out of the small box and slip it onto her slim ring finger.

'Sorry—I know it's kind of clumsy, but I wanted to surprise you and give you a lift, as I know you've had a stressful time of it with the McKlintoch business and hacking it out here alone. It's a harsh area for women on their own.'

Jessie was speechless. When Mack kissed her with deep passion, time froze—and the Palomino didn't take her eyes off them.

'Thank you for going to all this trouble, Mack,' said Jessie as she drew breath.

Mack searched her face with his wide hazel eyes.

'I hope you'll be happy living up here. We'll have to discuss it all with Grandad and see where he wants us to live. The homestead is big enough for all of us if you don't mind living there.'

'It's wonderful, I'll be very happy to live there.'

'But we need to discuss a date for a wedding. I was hoping in six months. That'll give you time to let your folks know and arrange for them to come down.'

'I suppose that sounds okay, but I need time to think about it.'

'Of course, I don't mind. But it would be great if we could let my folks know we're engaged, while they're still here.'

'Of course'. She turned and started walking towards the horse in the distance.

'I'll have to find a name for her, or does she have a name already?'

'I was going to leave that up to you', Mack said, as he approached them both.

It was as if the Palomino knew Jessie already. The mare shook her head and bumped her affectionately. Jessie reached into her jacket pocket pulling out an apple which Chantilly took from her.

'Here you go, girl. I'll be back to ride you soon—just you wait and see. We're going to be good friends. You're gorgeous.'

'Her name is *Chantilly*, delicate like lace and sweet like cream,' Jessie said, as she reached forward and rubbed the mare's nose.

'You can come here and ride her whenever you like. I'll take care of her until you are living on the station. It looks like Buster, our house cat has also taken a liking to you, the way she follows you around the house. Come on—we'd best be going back. Let's talk again tomorrow. I've got to go into the Farmer's Depot in Glenorchy to pick up some dry feed. I'll drop by late afternoon if that's okay with you.'

'That sounds like a good idea, as we need to talk about some things.'

'Are you ready for our announcement to the family? It's now or never. We don't have to confirm the date with them just yet.' He elbowed her and took her by the hand, leading her carefully through the long grass. Even though it was comforting to have her hand in his, it was a major adjustment to share her life with a man when she'd been self-sufficient for so long. Perhaps it was time to let go.

Chapter Twenty

The family had already gathered in the lounge when Mack and Jessie turned up. Before dessert was served, Meg and Joe were offered a beer by Walter while the others drank the rest of the chilled punch that remained.

'Well, what did you think of Reed Station? Was it big enough for you?' Mack asked his family, his eyes darting towards each of them. 'It takes a while to get around, doesn't it?'

Len answered first. 'It has certainly developed a lot since I lived here. We didn't have a dam in those days or solar power. Nor did we have those high-tech irrigation systems. The conifer trees you have as windbreaks were only saplings. You've certainly built the station up, Dad.'

'Well, that's what I'll continue to do while I can, thanks to good farm managers such as Aron and now, Mack. That's something I'd like to talk to you about—the future of Reed Station. Perhaps later this evening. Let's get into this food.' Jessie ascertained that the subject was uncomfortable for Walter to talk about and probably wanted to choose the right moment, after she'd gone home, perhaps.

Jessie's Pavlova, Bessie's traditional Christmas cake and the cheesecake Meg had bought, went down well. The women continued to sing Jessie's praises about her exceptional baking skills while she handed the plates around and sat down

'You'll make someone a great wife someday, lassie,' muttered Walter loudly, winking at her and making her cringe even deeper into her chair with the unwanted attention.

With that comment, Mack took it as his cue.

'Actually, we have our own announcement to make—Jessie and I have some news for you all.'

Everyone at the table sat holding their dessert spoons dead still and stared saucer-eyed at Mack then at Jessie.

'Jessie's accepted my hand in marriage today while you were touring the station.'

Their mouths changed from gaping holes to wide-brimmed smiles, especially Walter's. They all stood up and rushed up to congratulate them.

Walter, who was sitting between Mack and Jessie, immediately welled up with emotion. He leaned over and whispered with a croaky voice, 'I hope you aren't going to leave me now, Mack?'

Mack looked him in the eye. 'Not if I can bring my bride here and we can both share the house with you,' Mack whispered back to him.

Walter almost burst into tears of joy. A broad smile stretched across his face. 'Let's celebrate with some champagne!'

Mack grabbed his arm. 'Oh, Grandad, Jessie doesn't drink alcohol.'

'It's alcohol-free champagne from Cromwell, made from the finest white grapes.'

After they drank the champagne that Walter had kept for a special occasion, the family said their goodbyes to Jessie and excused themselves. 'We've had a big day and Walter wants us up early to tour the other half of the station. We'll be looking forward to seeing you at your wedding,' said Mack's mother, as the guests all went off to their rooms.

Jessie was overcome by all the excitement and wanted to have some time on her own to assimilate everything.

'I think I'd better get off now too. I'm a bit weary after today's activities. Can you come to my place for dinner tomorrow? We can talk about our plans for the future.'

'Sure can. I think it would be good to have some time on our own.'

'Come to my Land Rover and see what I got you for Christmas,' she said like an excited child.

Mack followed behind her and waited while she ducked into the back of the vehicle and pulled out a large package wrapped in red shiny paper. She handed it to him. 'Open it, please—before I go. It's something you had said you wanted.'

He opened the parcel on the roof of the vehicle and as the paper fell away, a black leather strap appeared then another. A brand new bridle presented itself.

'Wow! A brand new bridle for Zoro. His current one is completely worn and I need one for the dressage event in the next show. Thanks so much.' He leaned over and kissed her, this time taking even longer than he did when he had given her the engagement ring.

He slowly inspected the classy, black leather bridle with brass fittings designed for show events.

'This looks expensive. You shouldn't have. Perhaps you might like to keep it and use it on Chantilly.'

'Oh, no. I want Zoro to have it. He'll look gorgeous in this. Please take it.'

'I love it and so will Zoro. That's kind of you.'

'I'll be getting off now. I'll see you tomorrow. We have lots to talk about,' she said as she pulled herself up into her vehicle.

'I look forward to it, and I'll bring a load of firewood over. We need to make sure it'll last until you leave the cottage.'

He leaned through her open window to steal another kiss before she shut her driver's door then stood and waved her off.

As Jessie drove out onto the main road, she was surprised at how light the sky appeared. It was getting late. The sun had just disappeared behind the mountain range but a full moon lit up the road—a huge silver moon that appeared to smile at her. Tonight the stars appeared brighter than she'd ever seen before and she began to feel as though it had all been a dream, and she would wake up and find that none of it had actually happened.

As she opened the front door to her home, she realised that perhaps in six months' time she would no longer be coming home to an empty house—a bare property with no pets or a beloved horse. Her reality was soon going to change.

She sat in her armchair looking at her new sparkling engagement ring. Adrenaline rushed around her body at the thought of phoning her parents with the news. Then she decided to leave the phone call and surprise them at New Year with the good news.

Mack had slipped a photo of Chantilly into her hand before she had left Reed Station that day. It was as though it was a kind of magnet to encourage her to go and live at Reed station. She quickly shrugged off that random, suspicious thought, as she believed that Mack had much more integrity than that.

Tomorrow she would discuss with him how she would manage her veterinarian business while living on the station. Would he be expecting her to give it up to help her with farming? That was something she would need to clarify.

Jessie had worked up unwelcome anxiety about Mack's pending dinner date. She'd hoped it would be a relaxing romantic evening but now it seemed to have tension-building issues hovering over it like an ominous cloud. She prayed for peace of mind and courage to change the things she can, to be able to remain a strong independent woman as Mack sometimes unwittingly took charge.

***

That evening, Walter sat with his family in the lounge ready to have that discussion that he had hinted at having with them earlier—the subject of the future of Reed family estate, now that Mack was managing the station.

He got up out of his leather armchair. 'Anyone for a cold drink, or hot chocolate if you'd, rather?'

'Come and sit down, Grandad. I can get that if they want one. I thought you wanted to talk to us about the estate,' said Meg, as though she had an invested interest in what was going to happen to her share of the family inheritance.

129

'Yes, you're right. I'd better get onto that.' He took a worn-out handkerchief from his pocket, blew into it loudly and then stuffed it back into the pocket of his gabardine trousers.   –

There was quietness in the room. Joe began crossing and uncrossing his legs and Len sat erect clasping his hands together. Helen just peered out the window watching the large moon as it bobbed up behind the mountains. It was a clear, cool night, and the stars were sparkling diamonds—something city dwellers wouldn't see.

'You know that I wrote and told you that Mack has been managing the station since my longstanding Manager, Aron left. He has been a Godsend since my health has deteriorated and has shown himself to be competent and skilled in all aspects of sheep farming. Therefore I'm handing over the control of my estate to Mack with provision for Meg, a portion set aside for her on my death if the station is still making a profit.'

'I thought you had told me last night that the Trust was set up in such a way that it would always be kept as a working farm and would not be sold off,' said Len, frowning. 'That's why I had said I wouldn't want to benefit from the estate.'

'That's right. It will never be able to be sold off. That is stipulated in the Trust, but my will makes provision for Meg to even things out as Mack will continue to be Manager of the station.'

Mack just sat there watching the body language of the family members Walter had been addressing.

'That sounds okay to me. But what about you, Meg—are you happy about the situation? We don't want any red herrings thrown into the water later on.' Len nodded his head at her.

Meg gave her father an austere glance, frowning so much her nose-bridge wrinkled.

'I have another option you may not have thought about, Grandad if you want to make things equal between me and Mack.'

'Oh, I see ... go on.' Walter leaned forward resting his arms on his thighs and stared at her intensely.

'I have been thinking about how great this location would be for an exclusive country lodge. I could build one on the station. How do you both feel about it?' She bit her lip as she glanced at the men.

Mack, by this time also sat on the edge of his seat.

Walter spoke first. 'Absolutely no! I will never entertain the idea of running a tourist business on my station. This has been a sheep station for many generations and will not change. But Mack and I have another solution to the disparity in equity that you might have seen. Mack—you explain it.'

He glanced at Mack and nodded, giving him the go-ahead to talk, then sat back, clasping his hands like Len. He stared at Mack, waiting with tight, thin lips, ready to listen to him backing him up.

Mack's cheeks turned red. He undid the top button of his shirt as if it would make his breathing easier.

'I've been trying to sell my hundred-acre farm, as you already know. It has been on the market for several months now, but I've had no bites. That's mainly because of its remoteness. It will of course suit the right buyer, a local farmer. Nevertheless, in order to make my takeover of Reed Station fair to you, Meg —I've decided to gift my farm to you so that you'll be able to create the enterprise you want. The building which I have turned into a substantial farmhouse used to be an enormous barn and it's very solid. It will provide you with a good start. You can turn the land into grazing and lease it for locals who run out of feed. That will give you a supplementary income to support your project. What do you think Meg ... Joe?'

Meg was speechless for a minute. She sat there looking at her feet with a clenched jaw trying to work it all out.

'I think it's a pretty good offer, my girl,' said Walter. 'You can decide to run your boutique farmstay that will probably attract holidaymakers, or keep it on the market and sell it as a farm.'

'And I know you can get resource consent for the farmstay if you do go ahead, as my neighbours got one when they applied. But they sold up and moved away to Queenstown instead,' Mack added.

'Wow! I'm having trouble taking it all in. Joe and I need to discuss it first. What do you think, darling? Are you sure you want to leave Dad's business?' Meg asked Joe.

Len interjected quickly before Joe was able to say anything.

'Joe will have to have something to do when I retire at the end of this year. If you don't want to take over my company in Wellington, I'll sell it. If you are interested, I could be involved in the business side of your farmstay, just as we have already discussed. I just didn't expect to be doing it in such a remote area but I already feel the challenge. I think it'll be great.'

Mack was relieved that, in spite of the conflict and tension caused by Walter's decision to hand the station over to him the family meeting had a positive outcome.

'Perhaps we should all think about the propositions Mack and I have made this evening. Let's get together again tomorrow so that we can come to some sort of agreement before you all head off back to Wellington,' said Walter

They nodded in unison and went off to their bedrooms while Mack sat with Walter swapping feedback on how the evening went.

'Do think they were really happy with the solutions we came up with? I mean—you know your family better than I do now. We have become estranged all these years. What do you say, Mack?'

'I think Meg looked excited about the prospect of owning her own farmstay, and for years she has talked about how suffocating it was living in the city. It was Joe I was more worried about. I can't see him giving up the corporate business world to live in a remote rural area. But then again, I had no idea my father had decided to retire this year either.'

'Well, our prayers have been answered, Mack. God had made a way where there seemed to be no way. Let's pray about the meeting tomorrow and for Meg and Joe— that they will also come to know God as we know him.'

They bowed their heads and prayed that the outcome would be in God's hands.

Chapter Twenty-One

The next day, Mack arrived with a Ute full of firewood. As he approached Jessie's front porch, a delicious smell emanated from the house. She held open the front door.

'Hi there—by the smell of that lovely aroma wafting out the door, I'm sure I'm at the right house.' He removed his Stetson and pulled her toward him, kissing her more fervently than before.

'I'd better remove my boots before I come in.' He yanked them off and walked inside displaying his grey woollen socks full of holes. 'Whoops! You weren't supposed to see these,' he said, his neck flushing suddenly.

Jessie wondered if it was a hint for her to take them and offer to mend them. Then again, she barely had time to take care of her own clothing while she worked long hours as the area's only vet. What will he expect of her once they are married? This issue kept playing in the back of her mind. Perhaps he would ask her to stop her vet practice after the marriage. Was she having second thoughts? If not, why was she feeling so vulnerable?

'Come and sit in here.' She directed him into the lounge. 'It's cosy and warm with the fire going.'

'Mmm—I smelled the macrocarpa wood as I drove in. I have another load for you out there. How about I unload it for you first, before it gets dark?'

'Um ... okay, I suppose it's best. Let's have a coffee first though. I've got the kettle on and dinner will be a while yet.'

They sat and spoke small talk in front of the fire with their coffee then they both went out to the Ute. With the help of a wheelbarrow, they managed to unload and stack the wood just in time before the sun disappeared.

Minutes later, Jessie lay back in Mack's arms on the couch, trying to ignore a large toe poking through a hole in one of his socks. She chuckled.

'Something amusing you?' Mack poked her in the ribs.

'It's just your toe staring back at me. You sure have big toes.'

'Well, that's because I have a big heart!' They both laughed.

Jessie was almost lulled to sleep by the warmth of the fire and the strong, muscle-bound arm draped around her.

'Sorry,' she said as she suddenly pulled herself away. 'I'd better rescue dinner before I fall asleep.'

'Can I help?'

'No, honestly, there's nothing to do except dish it up. Do you mind if we eat here on our laps? I'll give you a tray.'

'Sounds very cosy to me. In fact, nice and relaxing. Just the mood to discuss our plans for our new life together.'

They both sat savouring the chicken and thyme hotpot with the poultry that Joel had given her on one of her visits. She only kept her own chickens for their eggs.

'Mmm, I hope this is a sample of what goodies I can expect when we are married. I'll have to sack Bessie and take you on as a cook.' He loved teasing her and this time she gave him a sharp elbow in his ribs.

'Ow! Okay, just joking. I know I'll have to keep Bessie on.'

'I need to talk to you about my vet practice—how I'm going to run it once I'm living on the station. I'm not sure what to do. I'll be too far away from Closeburn to be able to use the clinic there for minor surgery and other clinical procedures.'

'That's what I wanted to talk to you about. Do you remember we'd had the discussion about the possibility of you running a mobile clinic? You can buy a bus and have it fitted out as a minor surgery clinic and run your practice from Dart Valley. You won't need to buy a home now, so you can invest the money in the clinic.'

'But what about my clients on the other side of the lake in Kinloch?'

'I heard that Robbie Byrnes wants to extend his practice and offer more services south of Glenorchy. You can talk to him about it, in fact, discuss it with the Vet Co-op first. I'm sure they'll agree to you covering the whole of the Dart Valley out to Kinloch which is closer to home. That is a big enough area for you to manage on your own. If you withdraw your services from practising south of Glenorchy, they will have to find another vet and Robbie will do it.'

'It sounds good in theory. Where are these buses you are talking about?'

'In Queenstown. I can take you there when you get back from visiting your folks.'

'By the way—what was the outcome with your family, if you don't mind me asking? I mean Meg's request to set up a boutique farmstay on Reed Station?'

'No, I don't mind telling you, as it will affect you.'

He got up and took his tray and Jessie's out to the kitchen and came back and sat down.

'Grandad refused to entertain the idea. Instead, Meg and Joe have decided to take over my farm and set up the farmstay there. They'll use the land for local farmers to graze dry stock or they can lease it to a farmer. They may fence off a few fields as a mini-farm for guests to get close to animals. Meg has been keen to run ponies for children.'

'Meg with horses? I thought she was just a city girl.'

'Actually, she has been an experienced rider but not in the style that you and I are accustomed.' Mack knelt down to stoke the fire.

'Really—how's that?'

'They've been well-heeled, very well off. In fact, one of the elite couples in Thorndon. Meg has kept a few horses in stables there that she rents and has attended hunts with high-brow people in Wellington. I suppose one would call her a snob. But she had a few back problems and sold her horses several years ago.'

'Ah—so she's not the proverbial city slicker that I thought she was. I can see why she would want to keep horses then as a kind of compromise.'

'Yeah, she sounds pretty keen and my family support their move to my farm that I have gifted to her.'

'Oh, that sounds wonderful. How do your parents feel about the boutique farmstay?'

'They aren't bothered as my father has decided to retire this year. He has a lucrative business to sell and an upmarket home that will fetch a high price too. He and Mum are going to move to a small coastal town, probably to Nelson.'

'That's marvellous. It all appears to have gone smoothly then. What you thought was impending doom actually has worked as a blessing. Everyone is happy. See—I said that if we trust him, God will do for us what we cannot do for ourselves.'

They managed to get off the subject of the Reed family property and their finances and put the focus back onto themselves and their own future.

Mack pulled Jessie closer as she snuggled up to him. 'I was thinking that it might be snowing heavily by June or July. Don't you think we should plan the wedding later, perhaps in spring?' she asked.

'Actually, I was thinking of the same issue, only not about delaying it because of the weather but bringing it forward. What do you think about getting married in late April? I know it will be autumn but it will less likely be snowing heavily then and the weather is still stable,' said Mack.

'Goodness, that's in four months. I hope we can be organised then.' Jessie sat up erect and looked at him.

'I'm sure we'll manage, and we can hold the reception at Reed Station. Bessie will be a great help. I'll pay for your folks to come down and your brother, Tom as well.'

'Are you sure? I'd love that. But first I need to tell my parents all our news and let them have some input. They'll want to meet you first. Perhaps you can manage to tear yourself away from the station for a weekend,' said Jessie making him aware of her own needs too.

'I was hoping to invite them down here. There's plenty of room for them at the homestead and Grandad would like to meet them too.'

'I'll ask them when I go back home next week. I have lots to tell them and they are going to be a bit staggered, I would say.'

'Let me take you to the airport ... Monday, isn't it that you're flying out?'

'Yes, it is. Are you sure? I can ask Hope or Cole if they can take me.'

'No, honestly. I can use the trip to pick up some supplies in Queenstown. What time is your flight?'

'Eleven o'clock.'

'I'll be at your place at eight-thirty. That should give you enough time.' He flicked his wrist and looked at his watch.

'Great Scott! I didn't realise it was so late. I've got an auctioneer coming early in the morning to conduct a stock sale. I have to get the sheep penned up before he comes. I'd better get to bed.'

He kissed her and pulled her up on her feet, placed his Stetson on his head and walked towards the door.

'Leave me your holey socks. I'll repair them for you and you can give me any others that need darning. I don't mind, honest I don't.'

'Really, are you sure? I don't want you to think I'd be wanting you barefoot and pregnant as soon as we're married.' He laughed.

Jessie swiped him with a sock then threw them into the laundry tub, while Mack pulled his boots onto his bare feet.

'I'll see you on Monday. Thanks for the firewood. I really appreciate it.' Jessie squeezed his hand and Mack grabbed her around the waist and held her tight. 'I'm going to get used to these hugs real quick,' he said, winking at her as he turned and walked out to his Ute.

After he drove off, she had a sense of deep anticipation that was new for her—something she hadn't experienced all the years that she'd been alone. But now her hard-earned independence was starting to wane, and she was rapidly getting used to having affection and emotional intimacy fill a void in her life. She looked forward to Monday, the hour's drive with Mack to the airport. She already started fretting about having to fly to the Bay of Plenty and leave him behind. Her life had certainly changed.

Chapter Twenty-Two

The trip from Glenorchy to Queenstown Airport was pleasant—especially with the handsome, rugged chauffeur who was well-dressed in his blue and white check shirt and light brown suede trousers. Jessie was sure she could smell aftershave this time. The one that her father used to wear when he took her mother out for the evening. Her father, Wyatt was also a romantic. "Paco Rabanne"—that was the brand her father used. Fresh and spicy like cinnamon and vanilla. Expensive taste for a merino sheep farmer, she thought. Today Mack was clean-shaven and had his hair slicked back. Not with Brylcreem, but attained by a good brush.

He drove at a leisurely pace so he could talk. 'I have some news for you—something that will put a smile on your face while you're away.'

'Oh, really. What's that?'

'I told Grandad about you wanting to run a mobile vet clinic from Reed Station once we're married.'

'You shouldn't have told him that, as I haven't even got a vehicle to do it with.'

'No, wait. When I told him what your plan was to modify a minibus and turn it into a mobile clinic, he took me out to the large barn that he keeps locked all the time. He told me it was full of old vehicles and tractors that he doesn't use any more. You will not believe what was in there. A beautiful minibus that he had bought and turned into a motor home with the intention of travelling around when he retired. He had purchased it before he got sick the first time when he employed Aron as Farm Manager. It has been sitting in the barn unused ever since. It's a bit dated but in perfect condition.'

'Wow, that's amazing. Is he going to sell it?'

'No, he wants you to have it as a kind of engagement present—no strings attached. He has seen the need for a mobile vet clinic for years out here and feels he is making a contribution by giving it to you.'

As Mack turned to look at Jessie, large blobs of tears ran down her cheek.

'I can't believe how blessed I am. What a lovely generous man. Please tell him I'll be thrilled to be able to use it.'

'I have a good friend in Queenstown who is a mechanical engineer. He could probably modify it for you.'

'I can't wait to see it.'

As he waved to her from the departure lounge, she wished he was coming with her to meet her parents. Now she would only be able to describe him—his character and his appearance. Especially his character which was the most important aspect of Mack that she needed to focus on.

***

Prue and Wyatt Lee were overjoyed to see their daughter walk through the airport's arrival gate. Her mother rushed up to her, almost knocking her over with excitement.

'It's been far too long, Jessie. I almost forgot what you looked like. Goodness, how you've grown up so quickly. You're a mature woman now.' Prue kept fussing over her.

'Where's Tom? I thought he would be here too.'

'Your brother has had to watch the farm while we're away. There are ewes lambing right now and can't be left. He has almost finished his agricultural degree by distance study. We're so proud of him and your father has made him farm manager now that he is almost retiring.'

'That's marvellous. I knew he would do well. Anyway, Dad, where is my hug?' she asked, lurching forward at him as he wrapped his arms around his daughter. His smile didn't leave his face during the entire walk to the car.

'Wait—what's that on your finger?' her mother asked, as they were almost at the car. 'It's not what I think it is—or is it?'

Prue grabbed hold of Jessie's hand and stroked the diamond ring.

'Yes, I'll tell you about it in the car on the way home.'

As Wyatt swung onto the highway heading home, Jessie told her parents about Mack and how their relationship had developed. She went into great detail about Reed Station and her plans to operate her veterinary practice from there.

By the time they'd arrived at the farmhouse, Jessie had told the story about McKlintoch and how she'd finally won the battle for her credibility amongst the farming community

That evening, Jessie turned in early. She was shattered after the week's events. She looked forward to staying up to celebrate New Year's Eve with her family the following night, but right now she desperately needed sleep.

***

As Jessie snuggled into the bed that had always been hers, a strong sense of nostalgia soothed her. She realised that she'd missed her folks' farm and home. What troubled her was her mother's reticence about her being engaged to a high country farmer, so far away in such a remote place. Jessie really wanted her parents' blessing but now she wasn't sure that she was going to get it.

She recalled the conversations that had taken place earlier that evening. She had spoken to them about the events that had led up to Mack proposing to her and they didn't look happy. Prue had a constant frown and her lips were pursed. Wyatt kept looking down at his feet. Unlike him, his mood was flat. Tom had gone to bed early after working with the ewes all day, but he was the only one who appeared elated with the news of Jessie's pending marriage to a South Island sheep farmer. Tomorrow she would have to win them around, especially on New Year's Eve.

141

***

Jessie and her family didn't do much for New Year's Eve except go to the local beach to watch the fireworks display. Wyatt wasn't keen on fireworks except under strict control far away from the animals. The display had been put on by the local Lions Club and Jessie found it impressive considering Bethlehem was such a small community.

When they arrived home from the display, Prue made hot chocolate for everyone and they all helped themselves to freshly baked raspberry muffins and sat around the lounge chatting.

Prue brought up the subject of Jessie's plan to settle in Glenorchy and Wyatt took part as well. Tom did not want to interfere with Jessie's decision he told her earlier and took himself off to bed. 'Happy New Year, all of you. I think I'll turn in now. The lambs have worn me out the last few days.'

Jessie knew he was allowing his parents to have a good talk to her—the issue that needed discussing before she returned to Glenorchy.

Prue started first. 'I don't understand why a young woman like you would want to drive up and down on those dusty rough roads in an old beat-up truck to grumpy farmers, as you had described over the phone. And it can't be safe for you driving around those roads late at night visiting farms out in the sticks—not safe at all.' Prue's voice shook, and she appeared upset on the verge of tears. 'And Dart Valley is extremely remote, we've heard—miles away from anywhere, and there's nothing there. Not the life for a woman.'

'But that's what I've been doing ever since I moved there. I'm used to it now, and the vehicle is a sturdy, four-wheel-drive Land Rover, not beat-up at all. Anyway—Mack's not keen on me doing that anymore. He wants me to just focus my business on the Dart Valley area and not south of Glenorchy. The Co-op will have to find another vet for there. His grandad has a minibus that he had planned to use as a motor home before he had his first stoke. But after he suffered another stroke, he kept it in storage in the hope

142

that he would one day be able to tour around in it. When Mack told him I was going to buy a minibus to use as a mobile vet clinic, he said to Mack he would like to donate it to my vet practice, as there's a desperate need for a mobile service in the area. Mack's engineering friend is going to modify it for my use.'

Prue cupped her head in her hands and Wyatt slumped back in his chair with his arms folded tight.

'But remember that time you told me you had a flat tyre late at night and had to sit in your vehicle in the dark until some grouchy farmer turned up—the one who was a trouble-maker like that Doug McKlintoch.'

'I told you —I won't do that once I'm married. They'll have to get someone else to do the call-outs at night. Please, both of you. Come down to Glenorchy and see how beautiful it is, and you'll change your minds. Dad, you've got to see how such an enormous sheep station runs. You'll love Walter. He'll show you around and Mum— you and Bessie will get on so well. You can both fly back there with me this time. At least then you'll get to meet Mack's family before we are married.'

'We'll discuss it and let you know by the end of the week. We need to think about it. You'd better get some sleep, as you've had a big day travelling up here,' said Wyatt.

That night, Jessie was disturbed instead of being relaxed in the bed of her childhood. She really needed her parents' blessing and now was unsure if she would get it. The last thing she would want to do is to cause them pain. She was desperate.

Dear God—I don't know what I would do if I don't get my parents' blessing. Please speak to their hearts and persuade them to come back to Glenorchy with me. I know they'll love Mack and Walter. Perhaps we can all meet up with Mack's family in Wellington on the way too.

Jessie had pangs of guilt making such a request to God, as she knew he wasn't there to be used as some kind of Santa Claus. But she had a close enough relationship with him and knew he was loving and full of grace and would not want to withhold granting her hearts desires, not unless it was going to cause her harm.

***

At the end of the week, Jessie was all packed ready to return to Glenorchy. She'd accepted that she would be travelling alone again. Up until now, she'd decided that her parents were not showing any interest in her marriage to her high country farmer in the Southern Alps. But to her delight, she discovered she was going to be flying back to Queenstown with Wyatt and Prue in tow after all.5

They had surprised Jessie by saying that they had considered it carefully and had decided to keep an open mind. They also suggested she phone Mack to arrange for them to meet up with his family in Wellington on the way. That would involve two flights, and they offered to pay for her flight tickets to both airports. This marriage was already turning out to be a costly business, Jessie had decided, but these family details were important for her future happiness with Mack. But what if none of them gets along or they have a clash of personalities? The thought of it was too much for Jessie to bear, as she had always enjoyed a close and loving relationship with all her family members for whom she had much respect.

Chapter Twenty-Three

Tom stayed home to look after the ewes and lambs on the farm in Bethlehem. He relished the extra responsibility since his father had been preparing him to take over the farm once he decided to retire.

Mack had managed to arrange for his sister, Meg to collect Jessie and her parents from Wellington Airport. They were greeted with warm smiles as Meg and Joe met them at the arrival gate. Jessie sat squashed between Meg and her mother in the back of the car, while her father sat in the front talking about the state of the economy with Joe.

Jessie overheard her father saying to Joe that he was trying to decide whether it was time for him to retire. Why didn't he tell her that instead of her having to hear him tell it to a stranger?

Her parents' retirement was well overdue, she thought. They'd had children late in life and were both in their sixties.

'What will you do? I'd say it would be a wrench to give up farming after all these years,' said Joe.

'I had thought of selling the farm, but my son, Tom is keen to keep it going. He has almost finished his Agricultural Degree and is very up with the play. But I don't know what we'll do if we retire.'

Jessie sat half-listening to Meg chatting about her exercise and dieting routines while trying to catch on to every word her father was saying to Joe about their farm.

Joe tried to look cool driving his shiny, black Rover around the corners of Oriental Parade with a suntanned forearm leaning on the window frame. Jessie focused her gaze on the fancy Rayban glasses he was wearing.

'I've invited my parents over for dinner so you can meet them before the wedding,' said Meg to Wyatt and Prue. 'They'll love to hear all about the Bay of Plenty, as we had a few holidays in Tauranga several years ago.'

When they arrived at the two-story home in Thorndon, Jessie was blown away by their assumed wealth. The ostentatious home had a tennis court and swimming pool. How can a couple who live like this think that they can survive in a remote area like Glenorchy? Mack had told her that Meg and Joe had not wanted to have children. She said that they had far more important things to do with their lives. Jessie kept her opinions and concerns regarding this, to herself.

Jessie and her folks barely had time to relax before Mack's parents Len and Helen arrived and introduced themselves.

Later on, during the evening, Joe brought out all kinds of cocktails after a substantial meal, but he'd forgotten that none of them drank alcohol.

Meg explained to Jessie's parents that her brother, Mack had gifted his farm as her share of Walter's estate. Their grandfather had bequeathed it, in trust, to his grandchildren. Meg said that she and Joe were planning on turning the large home and ten of the one hundred acres into an exclusive boutique farmstay, but they were in a quandary about what to do with the residue of the ninety acres of grassland. Joe said that they might put sheep on it.

'You're an experienced sheep farmer, Wyatt, so I hear. What do you think I should do—do you think it could work?' asked Joe.

'I think it would be too big a job trying to run an exclusive farmstay which is a lot of work, as well as manage ninety acres with sheep. Even if you just used the land for grazing for another farmer, you would still need to maintain the fences, keep the weeds down, and fertilise the soil. There is also water to consider. Walter told me about the major droughts they've been getting in the last few years. You'd be better off employing someone to manage it for you and graze cattle on there, not sheep.'

Joe sat on the edge of his seat, leaning on his knees and rubbing his chin with his index finger. He didn't say anything for a few minutes, and then Helen passed around the cake she'd baked for them. Wyatt remained pensive and appeared to be mulling over the problem Joe was asking him to help solve.

Mack's parents stayed out of the discussion about the change of ownership of their son's farm. They preferred to keep their opinions to themselves, and Len had suffered enough heartache over family farms.

Joe lifted his head and turned to Wyatt who now sat awkwardly eating his cake with the dainty silver fork Meg had handed him.

'Wyatt—it's just an idea, and I may be barking up the wrong tree. But you mentioned you'd like to retire soon and take a step back. You said that your son, Tom is close to being able to manage your farm for you. What do you think about the idea of managing a smaller property such as our farmlet in Glenorchy? You can help us draw up a lease and manage it as grazing for other farmers. We will give you a good wage and we can build a separate dwelling for you and Prue to live in.'

It was as if someone had dropped a bomb. Everyone stopped what they were doing and stared open-mouthed at the two men. Jessie found her head spinning, as it was all moving too fast. She wasn't married to Mack yet and now all this was happening. But if it all worked out, she realised it would be a good thing. It seemed rational and logical, as her father was an exceptional sheep and beef farmer —but to imagine city slickers like Meg and Joe owning and running a farm seemed ludicrous.

This time Len spoke up. 'Think carefully, both of you,' he said nodding at Meg and Joe. 'It will be a huge upheaval after living here in the city and having everything at your fingertips. Not that I begrudge Wyatt and Prue managing your property—they are seasoned farmers and are used to living that way. Just discuss it carefully amongst yourselves before any of you make any commitments.'

Len was talking like a true businessman, and he'd been a good one at that. He was a level-headed man, much like Mack who was a chip off the same block. Jessie sat thinking how Len and Helen might be quietly feeling left out at the thought of all their family living in a remote community far away from them.

***

The next day, Joe spent hours taking Jessie and her family on a tour of the city by car. They returned home exhausted. He'd given a long and detailed history of every notable building in Wellington. Jessie was delighted they were only staying two days and couldn't wait to get back to the pure mountain air.

During the evening, they all took part in discussions about farming practices and the upmarket farmstay that Meg envisaged running. Jessie's mind was in another sphere. She imagined being married to Mack and having her parents living nearby. She wanted to see her father managing a small farm without having all the worry and responsibility of owning the business. But what if they move down there and find they don't like it? She would feel so bad.

'Don't you all think we should wait until you've had a look at Glenorchy to see if you like it there—I mean because it is so remote? I love it there, but you have to make sure it's what you really want and whether you can handle that isolated lifestyle.' Jessie was uncomfortable bringing it up, but she knew it had to be said, no matter how much she would want to have her family living down there with her.

'Well said!' Prue uttered, having not said a word the whole time. Jessie guessed that her mother was also facing the dilemma of considering how good it would be living so close to her daughter, and on the other hand, how remote it actually was living in Glenorchy.

They all agreed to wait until her parents had spent their holiday at Reed Station. They said that before their return to Bethlehem, they would make a decision. Tom would have to be happy with the arrangement too.

***

Mack had missed Jessie intensely but didn't let on when he picked them up from Queenstown Airport. She introduced her

148

parents then did her best to fill in the gaps in the lack of conversation as the Ute left the airport. She also guessed that her parents, especially her mother still had reservations about Mack, mainly because of the distance he would create between her and her daughter.

'Wow, look at that view! I had heard that the Glenorchy-Queenstown Road has some of the best views of Lake Wakatipu.' Prue rolled down her window to gape at the spectacular sight of the snow-capped Remarkable Ranges. The bright blue backdrop of sky cast a colourful reflection onto Lake Wakatipu. 'Can we stop for a photo please, Mack?'

'I sure can. It's beautiful, isn't it? One of the things that keeps me here. Wait—I'll pull over into this rest area along the road.'

Prue fumbled around in her handbag for her camera.

She stepped out of the Ute and walked to the concrete barrier, snapped her photos then stepped back into the Ute.

'That's why they call New Zealand *Land of the Long White Cloud*. See that long cloud that follows the mountains right along the Lake. When I used to travel south for my sheep shearing contracts, I often travelled along this road at sunrise. It was a majestic sight,' said Mack.

'That's so awesome. The scenery is breathtaking,' she replied.

Prue had shared something in common with Mack—a love of God's beautiful creation, part of the country's God-given heritage.

'There's lots more where that came from, Prue. Wait till we show you the mountains and lakes around Glenorchy.'

'Careful, I might just start to enjoy it,' she said, her eyes smiling at him. Even Wyatt leaned over her shoulder, gazing at the view. He appeared awestruck.

'Wait—we'll just make a little side tour.'

'Where are you taking us?' asked Jessie, tugging on his shirt sleeve.

'Ah, this is a little surprise for you too.'

As they drove along the lakeside towards Wilson Bay, Mack veered off to a side road. Jessie hadn't noticed the name on the road sign.

'What have you got up your sleeve?' she asked.

'Not long now, just wait and see. Wyatt, you're going to enjoy this one. It's right up your alley.'

The street led to another long private dirt road that wound its way through golden hills with dry yellow grass from the drought during this unusually hot summer. It appeared even more remote than Dart Valley. Mack drove slowly as sheep began to appear on either side of the road and before their eyes a lake suddenly appeared. Lake Moke popped up like a mirage, set against the yellow pinnacles. It was as flat and smooth as ice and the reflection was so perfect it looked like an artist had painted the background.

'This is unreal. What is this place?' Wyatt asked as Mack pulled over near the lake.

'This is called Ben Lomond Station—thirty-three thousand acres of grassland running seven thousand merino sheep and a few hundred cattle.'

'Well ... I've never seen a working farm this size in my life.' Wyatt just sat and scanned the peaks. 'Which one is Ben Lomond?'

Mack pointed to the mountain as he drove the Ute a little further.

'Look at the horses!' Jessie cried out, pointing at the horses at the side of the lake. 'Would they be wild?'

Mack laughed. 'No they aren't. They are working horses. Well looked after, aren't they? You can book a horse trek here on the Moonlight trail.' He turned the Ute around and headed back along the dusty road.

'Sorry, folks but the sight-seeing tour is over now. I have to get going as I have a few things to get ready before the morning. I have a stock agent arriving at eight.'

The mood in the vehicle was relaxed for the rest of the trip. Mack gave Wyatt a detailed rundown of the history of Ben Lomond Station and how it works. Prue was mesmerised by the awesome views of Lake Wakatipu, especially the range of blues in the reflections, repeatedly winding down her window and taking photos. Jessie sat back in her seat praying silently that the cordial relations between them would continue to flourish.

When they arrived at Jessie's cottage, Mack helped them with their suitcases and Jessie put the kettle on. He'd been looking after Jessie's house while she was away and unexpectedly placed a roast in the oven for her and her folks. Jessie had given him a spare key.

'Oh, wow! I didn't know you can cook. Especially as Bessie does all the cooking.' Jessie thought this was a real bonus in a prospective mate.

'Ah, not the case—sorry. Bessie cooked it early this morning and all you have to do is heat it in the oven.' He winked at Jessie and tugged her hair playfully while Prue whispered in her ear, 'No such luck! He's a farmer.'

Jessie was much more relaxed being back in her own home with her parents. She had not been at ease at the home of Meg and Joe, although they were kind and hospitable. Their lifestyle was so different from that which Jessie was accustomed.

Prue and Wyatt settled in and made themselves at home. After Mack returned to Reed Station, Prue told Jessie that her father had been quite taken aback by seeing the enormous Ben Lomond Station that was just minutes out of Queenstown. That trip seemed to unite the two men, a big plus for Jessie. And she could tell that her mother was impressed by her tall, rugged sheep farmer. They had hit it off well, she thought. Now to get both her parents to Glenorchy and see if the intrigue still draws them.

Before her parents turned in for the night, her father stopped to say goodnight.

'Before I forget, I want to give you this.' He pulled something out from behind his back. He handed her a cardboard box that had her name scribbled on the lid. She lifted it off and looked inside. There was her old straw rodeo hat and hidden underneath lay a pile of her satin, horse show rosettes and leather awards that she had won at rodeos.

'I thought you might still want them, and perhaps they'll be a little reminder of the good times you had growing up on our farm in Bethlehem.'

'Oh, Dad, that's sweet of you. Thanks for remembering to bring them down. That's the hat you bought me after I had won my first prize. I'll never forget—honest I won't.'

Prue overheard and walked into the hallway. 'I think he's really saying he doesn't want you to forget him.' She smiled, kissed her, and headed off to bed.

Jessie hugged him tight and walked into her office, making the excuse she had to finish some paperwork. She was trying to blink away the tears that forced their way down her cheeks at the thought of her father missing her more than she had expected.

Chapter Twenty-Four

The day after Wyatt and Prue had arrived in Glenorchy, Jessie drove them out to meet Walter who was waiting for them to arrive. He had put on his best clothes—probably the only set in his wardrobe and Bessie had left a casserole in the oven for them and gone out for the day. He paced up and down the veranda, waiting to greet them as they walked up to the front steps. He had even Brylcreemed his thin, grey hair.

Jessie rushed up and hugged the old man with whom she had bonded and was like a grandfather to her. He bared his new dentures in an overly full smile as Wyatt stepped forward to shake his hand, then Prue. He still hadn't got used to the new teeth he had made for him after his fall.

'Where's Mack?' Jessie asked as she quickly scanned the inside of the house.

'He won't take long. A ewe caught its head in the fence and he's gone to help it out,' said Walter as he ushered the entourage into his lounge.

'Mmm, something smells good through there.' Prue pointed towards the kitchen.

'Oh, that's my house-keeper, Bessie's beef casserole and I can guarantee it will be a hearty one. Can I get you a cup of tea or coffee? Or home-brewed ginger beer?'

'Oh, Grandad, let me.' Jessie jumped to the rescue. Since her engagement to Mack, Walter had asked her to call him Grandad.

He sat proudly talking at length about the history of Reed Station, how he had modernised the farm and built it up. Jessie was thinking about how insignificant his two thousand acres was compared to Ben Lomond Station.

Wyatt was intrigued by Walter's summary of the Reed family history and how he had single-handedly built up the station without the help of his family. Walter also went on to say how Mack had been his God-send and had come to his rescue. He told him how he had quickly shown himself to be a worthy successor to Aron, his previous Station Manager.

Jessie heard Mack's boots clunk as he tossed them into the corner by the front door.

'Oh, here's Mack,' she said gleefully, in the hope that he would rescue her from trying to keep a harmonious atmosphere between them. But she didn't need to. Her future seemed to be sealed in concrete already.

'Sorry to hold you up. I'll just go and wash up,' said Mack as he poked his head in the door.

'How about we eat after that, then you can take Wyatt and Prue on a Cooks tour of the station?' Walter nodded at Mack.

'That would be wonderful, Mack,' said Prue.

The substantial meal was followed by rhubarb and apple pie, with fresh cream from a neighbour's cow.

'Dear me, I hope I can still walk around after that lot!' Wyatt pulled at his leather belt and let it out a hole or two. 'Ah—that's better. I can breathe now. Tell Bessie I might take her on myself.'

Prue pulled a face of disapproval at him, playfully.

Jessie sat in the back of the Ute with her mother while the men chatted in front. It all went smoothly as if it was meant to be, she thought.

Half an hour later, as they were standing on the highest part of the station looking at the view of the expanse of paddocks and sheep, Prue turned to Jessie with a serious look on her face and spoke quietly. 'Mack and Walter are lovely. But the farmers in this area who have lived for years on these stations all their lives, have grown up with the remoteness and isolation. So different from where you grew up in the Bay of Plenty on a small farm near town. Are you sure you can live here like this? You'll only be able to do your grocery shopping once a fortnight, or even monthly. There's no doctor, and it takes over an hour to get to Queenstown on that metal road.'

Jessie clenched her jaw tight. Was her mother about to put the damper on her new life and, in spite of enjoying her stay, refuse to give Jessie her blessing? Perhaps her father thinks the same way. She watched him in deep conversation with Mack who was proudly pointing out notable aspects of the geography as far as Mt Aspiring National Park. To Jessie, her father appeared to be quite taken in by the enormity of it all and perhaps, not only interested but also impressed by the high country farmer who would soon become her husband.

'Jessie—I think we should take them up into Paradise and let them see the Red Beech forest in Mt Aspiring National Park. You don't have those up north, do you?' Mack asked Wyatt.

'No, I don't think so. We have English Beech trees but they aren't the red variety.'

'Well, our Red Beech is a native. It is abundant in the Mt Aspiring National Park as you'll soon be able to see.'

As they drove onto the Paradise-Glenorchy Road, they crossed a small river bed that was full of schist, a rock with blue-green hues that is quarried in Paradise.

'That is Arcadia Station over there and behind it is Diamond Lake.' Mack pulled up so that Prue could take more photos.

'That's where my friend Hope and I have ridden to on horseback. Isn't it beautiful?'

'Wait until I take you further up here. I can show you an amazing view of Mount Earnslaw. The weather is really mild for this time of the year. We can get out and have a walk around so you can photograph it.'

When they arrived at the spot that Mack was referring to, a flock of ducks appeared in front of the Ute.

'What funny looking ducks. They're goose-like. What are they?' asked Prue.

'They are called Paradise Ducks. The ones with the black bodies and white heads are the females and the males have green-black bodies,' said Mack as he continued driving up to a knoll near a clump of Beech trees.

'I thought that this place was called Paradise because it is like heaven here,' said Jessie, wide-eyed.

'No—that's what everyone thinks. It is named after these ducks.'

They stepped out of the Ute. 'Oh, that's a pity,' said Jessie. 'Because it really is paradise here. I didn't see as much as this on horseback. It seems different seeing it this way, and Hope and I didn't ride as far as this.'

'Wait until you see the view from up there,' Mack said, pointing at the grassy knoll. 'Are you happy about walking up there, Prue? It's only a short walk, but it'll be worth it.'

They followed Mack in single-file up to the top of the knoll. It was a wind-still warm day and not a cloud in the sky. As they reached the top of the small hill, there in front of them was a spectacular view of snow-capped Mount Earnslaw. Prue was mesmerised.

On the drive back to Glenorchy, Mount Alfred came into full view again.

'I've climbed that one—remember I told you I went up there with Mack, Hope, and Cole?' She elbowed her mother to jog her memory. 'That's the time that I slipped into a crevice and poor Mack rescued me.'

Mack turned his head and smiled at her.

'It was pretty difficult too, I might add,' said Mack, winking at Jessie.

'Oh, so you have been quite a hero in your day,' said Prue, beaming at Mack.

'Well, everyone. What do you think of Glenorchy? A touch of heaven, isn't it?' Mack chuckled as he came to the end of his tour.

Walter had been lying down resting when they arrived back at Reed Station. He got up and offered to make them a pot of tea.

'Sorry, Grandad, we're off out again. We've been invited for dinner with the Greys at Dart River Ranch. I'm sure their invitation included you.'

'Please thank them for me. I feel a bit tuckered out today and would rather stay home if you don't mind. I hope I see you, folks, again soon,' he said, glancing at Prue and Wyatt.

'Of course, they will. There's our wedding, remember?' Jessie looked at him with a querying glance, wondering if he really had forgotten about the wedding.

Jessie's parents said their goodbyes and Mack said he would follow them over to Dart River Ranch in his Ute.

***

Joel and Myra Grey hadn't seen Jessie and her family since she had left Tauranga to live in Glenorchy. They had more to do with them when Jessie and Hope went to the same school. That was many years ago.

Joel and Myra made a big fuss of them and before the meal, Joel took Wyatt on a guided tour of Dart River Ranch. Wyatt returned with a smile on his face and plenty of questions to ask Joel about running the ranch.

Prue was busy being entertained by little Bertie and finding out from Myra how she had found living in Glenorchy after leaving Tauranga. Hope took Jessie to the stables to see the new foals.

It had been a positive and uplifting evening and Jessie was more optimistic than she had been when her parents first arrived. Perhaps they had changed their minds, and she now had a concrete future in Glenorchy. But they still had a few more days to go.

Chapter Twenty-Five

On the way back to Jessie's cottage, her parents were quiet, probably fatigued after the grand tours that Mack had taken them on. He had organised with Wyatt to show them around his own farm, the one he had recently gifted to his sister. They would have to do that the following day as Mack had too much to do on the station after all that. It had been a whirlwind break for them down south. There was so much to see and do in such a short space of time. But Wyatt had a particular interest in wanting to see Mack's farm.

They were waiting at the gate of Jessie's cottage on the dot of eight the next morning, as the sun poked its head above the Richardson Mountains. The trees in the foothills were covered with a changing landscape of autumn trees—a myriad of pastel hues of orange, red and yellow.

Mack arrived rearing to go, wearing tan suede pants and blue and white check Swanndri. He climbed out of the Ute to greet Wyatt and Prue and helped them into the back of the vehicle.

'It's a bit chilly this morning when that southerly wind blows, even when the sun is shining. It's good you've brought jackets, as you might need them up on the ridge.'

Jessie climbed in next to Mack and kissed him on the cheek. As they drove to his farm, she placed a hand on his knee and Mack pulled her closer to snuggle up to him.

'Strap yourself in Jess. Here, let me help you,' he said leaning over with one hand, fumbling for the safety belt's port.

'It's okay—got it.' Jessie plugged it in then placed her hand over his weathered fingers.

As Wyatt and Prue were busy in the back talking about the different ranges of mountains they could see and naming the high country stations that they passed, Jessie took the opportunity to talk with Mack.

'We haven't had much time together with all this going on, sorry,' she said to him, screwing up her forehead.

'I know. I've missed you too. Never mind, they'll be gone tomorrow—shush.' He shook his head back to indicate her folks might be listening.

As they drove down the long driveway towards his old farm, a wave of sadness rolled over Jessie as the land appeared abandoned and neglected, although Mack had put a flock of sheep in the paddocks to keep the grass down. They got out of the vehicle and wandered down the path towards the house. Weeds were growing between the cracks in the footpath and at the front of the house thick cobwebs had meandered their way across the kitchen windows.

'It's sad to see no one living here after you've worked so hard to get it looking nice and homely,' said Jessie.

She turned to her parents. 'You know that this house was originally a massive barn that clever Mack skilfully turned into a lovely home. Can we go inside to take a look, Mack?' She pulled on his hand.

'Yeah, sure. I'll just grab the key. It's in my Ute.' He walked back to the vehicle while in single file they wandered around the perimeter of the house. Wyatt stood on the veranda looking out at the paddocks and scanned as far as he could see.

Mack showed them inside the house and then asked Wyatt if he would like to come with him on the quad bike he kept in the barn. He wanted to show him the rest of the farm while the women sat in the house talking about interior décor.

'Do you think Meg and Joe will be able to make something of this place, Jessie? It's a big house and the ground here is flat enough for them to extend it. But I just wonder if they will find it a mighty wrench after living in the city.'

'I think they'll be okay, Mum. Mack and Walter are family and they aren't far from here. Our church will probably help them, but it will be good if we can get them to come along to fellowship with us first.'

'Perhaps if your church helped them out here, they might warm to the idea of going to church. If they aren't churchgoers, it will have to be easy-does-it.' Her mother spoke wisely. She was always the one in the family who was the most level-headed.

'Mack told me that they are believers but have fallen away and haven't been to church for years. Mack and I have been praying for them, but Mack is concerned over their apparent materialism— that they won't be able to tear themselves away from it.'

The men arrived back on the quad bike and Wyatt appeared as happy as a sandboy flashing his off-white teeth. Prue rushed at him before he could get through the door. 'Well, what did you think of it?'

Wyatt brushed the mud from his boots and stood in the doorway re-adjusting his trouser belt. 'It's marvellous, so fertile. It's got all this flat land here, but if you go up on the ridge you'll see green, rolling hills that belong to the property. It's ideal for what Meg and Joe want to do,' he said.

'I'm sorry, but I can't make you a cup of tea or anything before we go, as I've emptied out the place,' said Mack with a sheepish grin.

'We can have one when we get back home. You've done enough for us, Mack,' said Prue, rubbing his shoulder with her hand.

'When you come down for the wedding, Meg and Joe will be here. That's if they can sell their own house by then,' said Mack.

'Mmm,' said Wyatt. 'That's going to be a great adventure for them. Wouldn't it be good to be young again?' He looked at Prue.

'What do you mean?' she asked. 'You've already been there and done that.'

'I mean taking on an enterprise like they are. It's a real challenge and sounds exciting. I don't know how they'll get on if they can't find anyone to manage the farming part of it. They have a perfect property here for sheep or cattle and it would be a pity to let it run down.'

'What about you, Wyatt, will you think about it?'

'I'm not sure. Prue and I will have to discuss it with Tom and see what he wants to do. I can't just abandon my own farm. It's something we'll all have to pray about, isn't it, Jessie?'

'I can ask our prayer team from church to pray if you like. They would be happy to do that, I'm sure,' Jessie said, uncertain if living on this property was the right course for them to take.

'I'll have to get you back home, as I have a few things to do before the day finishes. Hope you don't mind.' Mack rattled his keys in his pocket as a hint and made his way to his Ute with the others in close pursuit.

As they walked down the path, Wyatt kept looking back over his shoulder while Prue stopped to take photos.

'It's kind of sad to think we are leaving tomorrow,' Prue muttered in the back of the Ute. 'Time has gone far too quickly.' The corners of her mouth turned downwards as she pressed her face against the car window.

Was she actually imagining living here? Jessie wondered.

Chapter Twenty-Six

Over a month had passed since Jessie's parents had visited. Mack arrived to take Jessie out. They took off walking along a track on the Richardson Mountains overlooking the Rees Valley, talking about wedding plans on the way up the track.

'I can't believe it's March already. We are supposed to be getting married soon. It's gone so fast and we aren't even prepared. So much to organise. How are we going to do it all by then?' Jessie asked, pretending to pull Mack up the hill.

'I know what you mean. We've both been so busy since your parents visited and our feet haven't touched the ground. Don't worry— we'll work it out somehow.'

'Isn't that a lovely sight?' Mack pointed to the mountain range that appeared golden in the slowly setting sun.

Jessie stopped still to let the last rays of the sun gently warm her bare, swanlike neck. 'Have you heard my parents' news? I thought Meg and Joe would have told you. Mum phoned last night.'

Mack stared at her. 'No, what news?'

'Dad has accepted their offer to manage their pastures which will be leased out to farmers for grazing dry cattle. Meg and Joe are going to have a minor dwelling built for Mum and Dad which they will lease from them. It all seems to be happening very quickly so Meg and Joe must have been quite persuasive, seeing that they had seemed so convinced that Glenorchy was too remote.'

Mack stopped and pointed to a large flat rock. He led Jessie by the hand and urged her to sit down on it next to him.

'Let's stop here for a rest—it's all a bit sudden I guess. To be perfectly honest, I didn't really think your folks were that keen. Now we really will have to settle down together, won't we?' He looked at her and gave her waist a tug.

Jessie suddenly realised what the repercussions of all this would mean. It started to hit home what a great upheaval it would be for her parents to leave their own farm and start all over again in Glenorchy. *What if we did that and our relationship with Mack breaks up or we don't end up getting married?* She ruminated.

'I agree. I think it's all a bit rushed too,' murmured Jessie, pensively. 'Perhaps in view of all this, we should postpone our wedding until they come down. It would be better, as they should be settled in by then. What do you think?'

Mack shrugged his shoulders. 'I don't know. It's perhaps something you need to talk to your folks about again and find out exactly when they're planning on moving down. I think they may need more time to work it out.'

'I agree, I'll phone them tonight and let you know.' Jessie hauled Mack back up and urged him to get walking, as she wanted to take some photos of Mt Earnslaw from the top of the high ridge. When they reached the top, they saw the young farmer tenant waving to them from below as he repaired a fence by the entrance to the station.

'It's good he and his wife let us walk up here whenever we like. I've done a bit of contract work for him and we're good mates now,' said Mack as he waved back.

When they reached the edge of the ridge, Jessie took out her camera and got to work taking photos. 'I'm doing this for Tom, because he may not get the chance to come down here for some time yet while he is attached to my folks' farm,' she said, removing her sunglasses.

They sat down again, this time on an old log. Mack pulled out a chocolate bar and shared it with Jessie.

'Here—this will give you the energy to walk back down.' He chuckled.

'Don't you think it kind of complicates things that Mum and Dad are moving down here permanently because I've moved here? I feel for poor Tom running our farm on his own. And it all sounds so concrete. What if they get here and don't like it?'

'I think you're jumping to conclusions. Trust God—we've already prayed about it and now the outcome is in his hands.'

Jessie was aware that Mack didn't want to *rock the boat* when the wedding plans had been heading in the right direction.

'It's just that I'll feel really bad if they make a mistake and have to move again if it doesn't work out,' she said.

'It's the same for you and me. There's always a risk involved in commitment and you can be in exactly the same boat. Just wait and see what they say when you phone them. I'm sure it'll be fine.'

Nothing more was said. The weather was warm and Jessie was in her element as Mack walked the rest of the way with her hand in his, now and then giving it a gentle, affectionate squeeze. He showed a chivalrous streak by helping her over a stony stream or a rugged part of the path.

When they arrived back at the cottage, Jessie left her boots at the front door and waited for Mack to do the same. Instead, he took her in his arms and kissed her warmly, while still standing on the front porch.

'Sorry, Jessie, I've got to get back. I've been away all afternoon. I need to talk to Grandad about one of the irrigators that seems to be playing up. I won't be there when the mechanic arrives tomorrow, and he will have to handle it. Give me a call later and let me know how you get on with your parents.' He started to walk briskly towards his vehicle as Jessie followed behind.

'Oh, that's a pity. I have a chicken casserole in the slow cooker that should be just about ready.' Dashed hope sank to the pit of her stomach like a sack of potatoes.

'That's kind of you, but I told Bessie to keep me a meal.'

He placed his Stetson back on his head and climbed into his Ute.

As he drove off, Jessie was stunned. Had she said something during their walk that had changed his mind about her, perhaps? She realised she spouted on far too much about her parents not liking it in Glenorchy and the possibility of her relationship with Mack breaking up. Why didn't she keep her big mouth shut instead of verbalising her apprehension and wait until the process unfolds a little more? She thumped the dining table with a closed fist. 'You've done it again and put your foot in your mouth.'

Her voice still quavering from her upset, she picked up the phone and rang her mother.

'Jessie, lovely to hear from you. How are your wedding plans going? I had intended to call you tomorrow.'

Jessie turned her head to the side and coughed to clear her throat.

'Hi, Mum. We've got a lot to organise and think we might need more time. We may postpone it until spring to give you time to come down here.'

'Oh, really? I thought you might be all settled on Reed Station by the time we move. We were hoping to rent your cottage when you move out on your wedding day. I wanted to ask you to talk to your landlord.'

'Why is that? Aren't you moving onto Meg's property now?'

'Yes, we are. They are shifting down here next month and have already found a local builder to start on the chalet where we'll be living. It should be ready by the time you get married. You don't need to postpone your wedding for us.'

Jessie hesitated, trying to get her head around it all.

'Mack has tried to share his faith with Meg and Joe but they seem to be far away from God. That's just my concern if you are going to be living on their property.'

'Well, we are just going to have to pray hard for them. Perhaps that's the reason your father, and I have been led to move onto the farm with them. God will change their hearts—just you wait and see. Even if it takes years, he will succeed.'

Everything seemed to be moving so fast, but she didn't want to dampen her parents' plans.

'If it's convenient, we'd like to stay with you until you move onto Reed Station after you are married. Please speak to your landlord first and let me know if he'll transfer the tenancy over to us.'

'Sure, Mum. I'll phone him tomorrow. It'll be nice to have your support for the wedding. I just hope you'll be happy down here. Otherwise, I'll feel really bad if you aren't.'

Prue continued to reassure Jessie that she and Wyatt both desired a change and Tom needed the responsibility, as he had become a man. She prayed a short prayer over the phone and hung up.

As Jessie was about to leave the office and walk into the kitchen to put the kettle on, the phone rang again. Why would her mother be phoning her back?

'Jessie—it's Mack. Have I caught you at a bad time?'

She was taken aback that he was phoning so soon. It must be urgent.

'No, not at all ... is everything alright?'

'Ah ... yes ... sort of. I have a confession to make ... you see I really did want to stay for dinner when you asked me in but when I kissed you I had stronger feelings for you.'

'What do you mean—that's normal, isn't it?'

'What I'm trying to say is ... the kind of feelings that are best left at the doorstep. I was caught off guard because of the fun time we had on the walk today. I respect you and our mutual agreement to wait until our wedding day.'

'I'm so relieved to hear you say this. I was so worried I had said or done something to put you off me. The thing is ... I feel the same way about you. I have loved you so much ever since you pulled me out of that crevice on Mount Alfred.'

'You're a darling. Why do you think I kept asking Hope or Cole when you were coming back to Dart River ranch again? I can't stop thinking about you. We've got a lot to talk about and to plan.'

Jessie perked up after that conversation with Mack and the next day they discussed their wedding plans together as they didn't want to put it off any longer. They decided to plan for late April, that time of the year when the snow caps on the mountains make a perfect backdrop for photos and the weather is still warm enough for a garden party reception. If her parents moved in with her, that would make life easier—then after she moves to Reed Station, they will be able to stay in the cottage. Perhaps this is all part of God's plan. She stoked the fire and gave it no more thought until the next day.

Chapter Twenty-Seven

Lance, Jessie's landlord was more than happy to give the tenancy over to her parents. He and his wife, Mary had both met them during their visit to Glenorchy and they got on well. After Jessie had let her parents know, she phoned Mack.

'That's great news, Jessie. All sorted then! Oh, by the way—Meg rang me last night to say that Briars Property Development will be starting the build on your parents' cedar chalet next week. It should be ready in a few months. They are moving down in a month. Their house is on the market but may take a while to sell.'

'Well, that's all settled then. It's kind of exciting, I suppose.' Jessie caught herself, realising how that must have sounded.

'You don't sound so convincing, but you just wait and see— everything will fall into place. I have a good feeling about it all.'

Six Weeks Later

It has been a long, hot summer, and although autumn had arrived, it was unusually warm.

Wyatt and Prue piled into Jessie's Land Rover ready to drive out to Meg and Joe's new property, Willow Park. They appeared excited, as the outside shell of their new chalet had been completed—an attractive, Swiss-style chalet with a concrete path leading to it at the back of the boutique farmstay. Meg and Joe had already moved into their home. They'd arrived earlier than expected and were hard at work outside clearing away weeds and shrubs ready to create a new garden.

As Jessie drove up to their house, Meg stood up and waved. Instead of her chic, elegant Hartley's attire, she wore faded denim jeans, black tee-shirt, and muddy gumboots. Her hair was in disarray.

'Mmm, maybe she is cut out for rural life after all,' Prue muttered to Jessie.

'It's possible. She said she always loved holidays in the country, so who knows? It may suit her.'

Prue and Wyatt were over the moon about their home taking shape. It was far enough away from the lodge to give them plenty of privacy.

Afternoon tea with Meg and Joe was on the agenda. After they had finished, Joe took Wyatt up to the back of the farm to discuss their plans while the women looked at Meg's décor books for ideas for the farmstay. With Prue and Jessie in tow, Meg did the rounds of every room in the large house then led them out onto the patio where they sat and chatted until the men returned.

'I went to my first Country Women's Institute meeting a few days ago. It was not what I expected. I thought they just sat around showing off their knitting and preserves, but there were some speakers—professional women discussing the changes going on in women's roles in farming and local politics.'

'That's nice, dear. I'm glad you're getting involved in the community. We all need support and you can make some friends there.'

'I'm not so sure now. I may have upset some of them. When I told a few of the women about my boutique farmstay, they frowned and murmured amongst themselves making me feel really uncomfortable. The speakers had been talking about their opposition to all the housing development that has been going on in the area—farmers being offered large sums of money to have their farms subdivided into smaller properties. I wish I'd never told them. I was just trying to drum up some publicity for our new venture.'

Prue, who had been a long-term, staunch member of the Bethlehem branch of the Institute, pulled a straight face and bit her lip.

'I'm sure they'll warm to you once they get to know you better. Maybe if you show them your farmstay and invite them around for afternoon tea, they'll become more accepting of you.'

After the tour of the property, they were all busy on the trip back home, chatting about all that was going on with Meg and Joe's farmlet.

***

Jessie terminated her employment with the Vet Co-op a month before the wedding. It had not taken long for them to find a replacement this time, much to her delight. Some farmers who lived near Reed Station had told her they would continue to use her services, particularly her private mobile clinic.

Everything appeared to be falling into place, just as Mack had suggested, thought Jessie. This was only the beginning, and they had a long road ahead before their new lives in Glenorchy would show promise.

Chapter Twenty-Eight

A High Country Wedding – autumn 1980

April arrived faster than Mack and Jessie realised and the weather remained dry apart from snow on the mountaintops. They'd planned a simple country wedding on Reed Station, and although they had tried to keep the guest list to a minimum, it just seemed to grow. There were so many local people they couldn't leave off the list.

Tom had arrived the night before. Cole and Hope had driven to the airport in Queenstown to collect him off his flight and Cole kept him busy showing him around their ranch after they arrived home.

Jessie's parents stayed with her at her cottage and Meg invited her folks to stay at Willow Park. She wanted her father to help set up her business accounts before they returned home to Wellington. He was the one with the tax accounting skills.

All the ladies, including Jessie, were hard at work helping Bessie the day before the wedding, preparing the colonial homestead which the men had whitewashed. The crimson carnations and mauve cineraria were in full bloom and the women had cut many of the blooms and placed them in a bucket of water ready to be made into bouquets and posies mixed with white gypsophila. They laced miniature dark red roses together to form a chain to drape around the railings on the veranda.

Walter had made sure his station hands would be able to sit at a table and share in the wedding breakfast, as they were part of the family. It was a way that Walter showed his gratitude for their long-term loyalty.

After dinner that evening, Prue was busy in her daughter's bedroom sorting out her bridal gown and accessories. Jessie had arranged for one of the local farmer's wives to arrive early on her wedding day to fix her hair. Everything was running to plan.

'Tom—while you're here for the next few days, it would be a good idea to ask Walter if he'd give you a tour of the station. The sheer size of it will blow your mind,' said Wyatt, tousling his son's hair with his hand.

'Sorry everyone, but I'm having an early night. I've got to get to bed,' said Jessie, walking into the lounge to kiss her father.

'Night, night, sleep well.' Tom called out from the hallway. 'I'm turning in too.'

Prue was in Jessie's bedroom doing a last-minute check of the crème, Chantilly lace bridal dress, and headpiece of white satin flowers. Jessie startled her. 'Ah! Don't creep up on me like that. Just making sure you have everything ready for tomorrow.'

'Sorry—thanks, Mum. I'm exhausted. Need to get to bed, as we have to be there by eleven. The Pastor will be starting the ceremony at twelve.'

'No, you can't let Mack see you until the wedding. Meg, Mack, and Joe will be able to set everything up and Bessie will be there too. Your father is going to drive us there in time for the start of the ceremony.'

'Aw, thanks, Mum. You're an angel. I'll see you in the morning.'

'Wait—let me say a wee prayer before you go to sleep.' Her mother sat down on the bed next to her. She took her hand and asked God for guidance and protection and that everything would go smoothly for Jessie's special day.

***

The station hands set up a large marquis and trestle tables which Bessie covered with long white tablecloths. She and a few other ladies placed mini, dark red roses in small vases. It was not a formal affair. Most celebrations in the area were usually laid back and involved the whole community.

All their neighbours and church parishioners had offered to bring food and started slowly arriving, taking the food into the house for the women caterers to prepare to put out on the tables later.

Pastor Johanne waited in the front garden by the lily pond, while the guests sat patiently waiting to see Mack and Jessie appear.

As they all looked around to see from which direction the bride and groom were arriving, the sound of a horse clip-clopping down the track drew the attention of the crowd. At the same time, beautiful music wafted in the breeze towards the guests who looked around to see where it came from. It was the harmonious tune to the wedding song *I Will Always Love You.* It emanated from the veranda as Walter walked out the front door playing the fiddle. He was dressed in a sophisticated woollen, marine blue suit with a navy tie. His thick grey hair had been washed and styled. The guests stared open-mouthed as he continued to produce awe-inspiring music.

Suddenly, as if from nowhere, Mack appeared on his beautiful black stallion. Zoro walked steadily towards the bridal party and stopped by the Pastor. Mack was wearing the same style of suit as Walter, who stopped playing and stepped up beside him as best man.

Zoro appeared to be showing off, with his tail swept up in a blue band. His mane had a blue ribbon braided through it. The animal just stood there as still as a queen's guardsman. The black horse contrasted with the backdrop of snow-capped mountains in the distance. He was harnessed in the new black bridle that Jessie had gifted to Mack.

It was the first time that Mack had heard his grandfather playing the fiddle. He had simply not expected to feel so overcome with the emotions that flooded his mind and his eyes with salty tears. He had not known that Walter could play like this, as he had had told him he had stopped playing after his first stroke some years earlier.

***

Wyatt and Prue had furtively arrived in the Land Rover with Jessie in the back and stopped around the back of the barn. They were busy helping her to make a surprise appearance on horseback. When she was ready, Prue went over and sat next to Helen and Len on the seats provided for the bridal party and started chatting to them. She was wearing a pink and grey, flared chiffon dress with a tight bodice, and carried a pink clutch bag.

As suddenly as Mack had appeared, a stunning golden Palomino carrying a radiant bride appeared from out the back of the barn with Jessie sitting side-saddle. Her dress, made of exquisite Chantilly lace fell elegantly in layers covering the saddle and the side of her mount.

The well-preserved saddle was one that Walter had kept in the barn all these years in memory of his wife Hazel. He'd offered it to Jessie for the wedding and spent hours polishing it up and shining the silver buckles for her.

As Chantilly approached the gathering near the homestead where the guests were seated, Jessie was suddenly distracted by a bright blue object amongst the guests. She caught sight of Meg who was walking down the steps of the house simultaneously as she was arriving. She stuck out like a sore thumb, standing on the lawn preening herself in a royal blue, satin dress and white, stiletto-heeled shoes. Her long, blond hair was swept up and on top of her head was a large, flat, blue disc, a hat that appeared as a flying saucer covered in blue netting to match her dress. There was another layer on top with several miniature flying saucers hanging over the brim. It was a though she was trying to look like one of the Royals.

Jessie sat open-mouthed. Meg was trying to steal her thunder. Joe appeared to be embarrassed, pulling at his tie, and running his fingers through his hair. He pulled on Meg's arm, trying to get her to sit down.

With Wyatt at her side, Jessie urged Chantilly on towards the spot where Mack and Zoro waited. Wyatt held the horse's cream coloured bridle and reins which matched her dress. He had come to give his daughter away. Chantilly threw her head in the air as if to make a statement then came to a halt next to Mack, who sat still in his saddle staring at her and beaming from ear to ear.

He leaned over and squeezed her hand. 'You look radiant, a real picture in all that lace on top of Chantilly.' Mack lifted off his dark brown leather Stetson and bowed at his bride.

Chantilly's mane had been intricately braided in a pattern that resembled Chantilly Lace with miniature dark red rosebuds interwoven. Her tail had been decorated in the same fashion. The guests started photographing the amazing spectacle before the horses became restless.

At last, the Pastor started the ceremony with Hope standing alongside Jessie as Matron-of-honour and Wyatt on the other side. Walter now stood next to Mack as his Best Man holding onto Zoro's bridle.

The guests were entertained by a little pageboy—Bertie, Hope Rigby's son. He stood next to Mack's faithful dog, Bluey on the bottom step of the veranda wearing dark blue pants with a midnight blue waistcoat and red velvet bowtie. Bluey sat patiently, showing off a similar red bowtie.

Bertie held a small, red velvet cushion that housed the rings. He was pleased as punch that he played a part and stood there babbling baby talk. His father, Cole supervised him while the guests laughed. The small boy leaned over to place the cushion on the step and as he went to sit down on it, Cole snapped up the rings in a panic. That brought forth another outburst of laughter while Bluey gave a loud howl like a coyote and joined in.

It was a simple but powerful event with a strong message. The Pastor preached about the power of love and forgiveness. Walter's eyes stayed moist for almost the whole of the wedding ceremony.

The event was doubly emotional. With their final tying of the knot, Walter and his grandson, Mack had healed a long-standing generational feud with Jessie's help.

Jessie and Mack had both agreed when they had been planning their wedding, that they would write their own vows. Of course, they had to get Pastor Johanne to look them over so that he was in agreement. When they each read out the words they had written, they were said with deep sincerity as they looked into each other's eyes.

After Pastor Johanne had announced them, *man and wife*, Mack lifted Jessie off Chantilly's back carefully so that she wouldn't damage her delicate lace dress. He pulled her close and kissed her more passionately than ever before until the Pastor nudged him to say that the ceremony was over, as he wiped the steam from his spectacles. When Jessie looked at the crowd, she saw that what had taken place had brought tears to many eyes.

Mack stopped Jessie from walking off so that he could get a good look at her. Even though the Chantilly lace she was wearing had matched the colour of her mare's coat, she had stood out beyond description. She had grown her thick, flaxen hair a bit longer for her wedding and Walter's neighbour had styled it for her and set it in long ringlets. Her cheeks were rose pink because of the anxiety she had experienced during the ceremony, but her facial colour also contrasted with the colour of her dress. On her feet, she wore dainty, flat, cream-coloured satin shoes. A far cry from the heavy leather boots she wore each day to work.

She had always wanted to get married on horseback, a quirky dream of hers and it had come true. Mack was her Lancelot, and she was his Guinevere. He pulled her close again and kissed her neck.

Tom had offered to take care of their horses before and after the ceremony. He was proud to be of service to his sister that day. He had dressed smartly in the same attire as Walter and Mack. The station hands also joined in with the guests for the rest of the occasion, eating, drinking, and accepting Mack and Jessie's hospitality.

One of the guests managed the roast lamb-on-spit and Tom proudly handed around refreshments. Bessie provided last season's ginger beer and there were some fine Marlborough wines for those who wished to partake. Seats lined the walls of the marquis that had been ornately decorated.

Several women started to go back and forth into the house and out to the trestle tables bringing an abundance of savoury dishes to go with the roast meat. This was followed by rich desserts fit for a king, such as Black Forest Gateaux, Chocolate-pineapple cheesecakes, Pavlovas covered with strawberries and cream, huge chocolate logs and trifle.

Joe, as the master of ceremonies, headed up the toasts after he had read out the telegrams. They raised their glasses as Joe spoke— 'To the bridal party and our supportive community for making this such a happy and memorable occasion for Mack and Jessie, that it has turned out to be.'

At the end of the toasting, they were entertained by a singing telegram that had arrived for the bridal couple in the form of an Elvis Presley impersonator singing *Crying in the Chapel*. For Jessie, this was the highlight of the wedding reception.

The emcee announced the cutting of the cake that sat on the Sweetheart Table. The four-tiered cake had been made by Jessie's mother, Prue—a traditional rich, dark fruit cake with imitation miniature purple roses. On the top tier of thick Royal Icing, stood a bride and groom on horseback.

Walter handed Mack and Jessie his late wife, Hazel's elaborate silver knife to make the traditional first cut of the cake. Hazel had been an accomplished cake decorator and Walter had kept it as a memento. Jessie and Mack placed the first slice on a plate and fed each other a mouthful with small forks. Prue then took over and gathered up the top tier—it was a tradition in her own family to freeze this until it was required as a Christening Cake for a firstborn child or a first wedding anniversary.

The rest of the cake was left to a couple of young people to hand around to the guests after the bride and groom had each taken a slice to the bridal table.

***

There was still a chill in the air, and instead of the dance being held outside in the marquis where they had been eating, Mack decided they should move into the big barn. His station hands had put up the coloured lights around the inside walls earlier that morning to brighten it up and placed more chairs borrowed from the church to put around the dance floor.

177

Of course, Walter provided the dance music along with one of his ranch hands, an accomplished musician like Walter who played the piano accordion.

Jessie watched her brother, Tom closely when he was dancing. She knew it wouldn't be long before some sweet girl would whisk him off his feet and marry him.

Meg gave a few performances demonstrating her trained, angelic voice, once again soaking up the limelight.

'Remember I'm still waiting for that last dance that I didn't get at Hope's twenty-first birthday party or her wedding. I've been waiting ever since.' Mack cupped Jessie's face in his hands as she melted.

'You're kidding, aren't you?'

He kissed her softly and kissed her again.

'No, really. I was thoroughly disappointed when I was trying to impress you way back then. I had to wait a long time for you to return to Dart River before I could try to win your heart.'

Jessie's face turned pink. 'I'm sorry. It wouldn't have been on purpose. I think I was called away to help Myra prepare the supper at her twenty-first, then forgot you were waiting. As regards her wedding, you just weren't quick enough off the mark. Someone else beat you to it!' They both laughed.

'Well, I'll never have to wait again, will I?' He chuckled. 'Let's dance the night away.'

'You know something ... all our prayers seem to have been answered. It's amazing isn't it?' Jessie wrapped her arms around his neck as she danced and snuggled into his neck.

'It does seem we've been in God's will, even when it didn't feel like it. So, what do you think—will you be staying on in remote Glenorchy, grumpy farmers and all?' He poked her in the ribs and smiled.

'I can't imagine going back to town. It appears that this is my divine purpose. You and I can make a real go of it. Let me help you run the station, and I'll work at my vet business part-time. Once my mobile clinic is up and running, I won't be doing any more after-hour calls, now that they have a new on-call vet.'

'Really, that's great news. A husband and wife partnership. You'll have a heap of work to do caring for our own farm animals with a thousand merino sheep, four hundred cattle, dogs, and horses—then there's me, of course,' he said, his eyes gleaming playfully. 'Oh, don't forget Grandad too.'

'That's what I realised. I'm rather looking forward to it. I made up my mind after you gave me Chantilly, that I can now do what I've always been cut out for—that is, working on the land. I miss it … I miss riding.'

When the music stopped at the refreshment interval, Mack took Jessie's hand and led her outside to look at the sky. It was so clear it seemed as though she could reach up and pluck the sparkling stars like diamonds from the heavens. The brightness of the imposing silver moon gave the illusion of being able to warm her, on this crisp, autumn evening. She shivered. 'I should have wrapped my shawl around my shoulders. I left it inside.' She rubbed her hands up and down the top of her bare shoulders.

'Come and sit down over here. I'll keep you warm.' He pointed to a wooden bench at the side of the barn. He took off his jacket to reveal a white shirt with long sleeves. 'I'm lucky I've got a thermal under this. Here—this will keep you warm.' He wrapped his jacket around her shoulders.

'Do you hear that? It's someone else playing the fiddle.' Jessie was leaning over peering through the entrance to the barn. 'It's the Pastor—he can play too. He's playing a tune so that Grandad can dance. Take a look.'

Mack leaned over Jessie to see Walter dancing with Meg. Then he saw his parents dancing next to them.

'It's one of Grandad's favourites called, *My Heart Will Go On*, the Titanic theme.' Large globules rolled down Mack's cheeks. 'It's hard to believe that it took our marriage to break the icy hearts of my family and dissolve the feud that has kept us all apart for so many years.'

It's just as you told me that time when I was about to give up— when all the odds seemed against me. You quoted that verse from the Bible— '*But seek first God's Kingdom, and his righteousness and all these things will be given to you as* well'.

***

The honeymoon on Coronet Peak zoomed by far too quickly for Mack and Jessie. It was Walter's wedding present to them. He had even booked them into a honeymoon suite in a fancy Swiss chalet.

Not far from there was Arrowtown, a favourite place of Mack's. That's because it exhibited many photos and articles about Mack's ancestors in the little museum there. He loved the fact that a sheep shearer called Jack Tawa first found gold in Arrowtown.

They could only spare a week away from the station, as they couldn't leave Walter with all the responsibility. They had asked Wyatt and Prue to help out, although the station hands were reliable and responsible. At least Jessie's parents didn't have to go all the way back to the Bay of Plenty, as their chalet was already completed and they had settled into their new home. Tom had returned to the farm in Bethlehem and was coping well.

Chapter Twenty-Nine

They were at last settled in at home on the station. The snow was now low lying and the view from the veranda of their homestead was spectacular. The newlyweds sat on the wooden seat looking out at the mountains. The pinnacles glistened in the late afternoon sun, which cast a myriad of pastel hues over them with shades of pink and mauve.

Jessie pulled her merino shawl tighter around her shoulders as Mack slipped his arm around her slight waist and pulled her closer.

'You know—when you were having all those awful ups and downs trying to break into the farming community, I have to say, I did despair a few times. I thought you would shoot through never to be seen again. I'm so glad you stayed.'

She leaned over and kissed his cheek. 'It wasn't me who kept me here. God did for me what I couldn't do for myself. He put the desire in my heart and gave me the strength and courage to overcome.'

'I know he did. He certainly made a way where there seemed to be no way. Look at how everything has come together.'

They continued to sit watching the changing horizon as the sun was going down. Jessie Reed had become a high country station manager jointly with Mack, and the new on-call vet had already started work. Now she would be able to help Mack run Reed Station, as well as work part-time running a few clinics each week. She had it all—the handsome farmer, her family around her and the mountains. Jessie had been so blessed, and she was determined to make a real go of it. The high country was her home, and she was here to stay.

Chantilly appeared at the fence watching them.

'Oh, okay Chantilly, I'm coming'. Jessie picked up the bucket of oats she had ready for her on the veranda and turned to Mack.

'I can see what you or someone has written on her cover. That's sweet of you.'

As she drew closer, she read the words painted on the horse's cover—*Jessie Reed—just married!*

She looked back at Mack who sat on the veranda grinning. Chantilly whinnied and nudged her with her head as if the intuitive animal knew exactly what was going on. Jessie's heart melted. It was as though her life was just about to begin all over again.

******

If you have enjoyed this novel and it has warmed your heart, please leave a review on your preferred reading platform.
Check out my website and join my mailing list. I can keep you informed about the next book in this series, my new releases, and giveaways.

I love to keep in contact with my readers.

Website: www.patriciasnelling.com